MANDIE®
AND THE GHOST BANDITS

Lois Gladys Leppard

BETHANY HOUSE PUBLISHERS
MINNEAPOLIS, MINNESOTA 55438
A Division of Bethany Fellowship, Inc.

Mandie and the Ghost Bandits

Library of Congress Catalog Card Number
84-71151

ISBN 0-87123-442-4

Cover illustration by Chris Dyrud

Published by Bethany House Publishers
A Ministry of Bethany Fellowship International
11400 Hampshire Avenue South
Minneapolis, Minnesota 55438
www.bethanyhouse.com

Printed in the United States of America by
Bethany Press International
Minneapolis, Minnesota 55438

In Loving Memory of
That Dearest of All Fathers,
James William Leppard
(1886–1960)
Who Taught Me What Books Are,
and
My Dear Brother,
Arnold O. Leapard
(1909–1975)
An Artist of Great Renown,
Both of Whom Have Gone on Before,
And Both of Whom Led Me Along the Way.

About the Author

LOIS GLADYS LEPPARD has been a Federal Civil Service employee in various countries around the world. She makes her home in South Carolina.

The stories of her own mother's childhood are the basis for many of the incidents incorporated in this series.

Contents

Chapter 1 / Journey on a Train

In the dark alley behind Bryson City Bank, Mandie Shaw stood on tiptoe to peer over the side of the wagon. Her heart beat faster at the sight of the small leather traveling bags full of gold nuggets.

Mandie's Uncle John and two Cherokee Indian friends loaded bag after bag of gold nuggets into the wagon while Mr. Frady, the short, round banker, watched nervously.

Uncle Ned, Mandie's old Indian friend, plopped two bags of nuggets into the wagon. "Gold bad for Cherokee," he mumbled.

Mandie, with her white kitten, Snowball, on her shoulder, took Uncle Ned's hand and returned with him to the vault for more. "But Uncle Ned," she said, "just think what a wonderful thing we are going to do for the Cherokees with all this gold. Something that could never be done without it. We should be thankful for finding it in the cave."

"Humph! Gold not good for Cherokee," Uncle Ned insisted. "Better left in cave."

"But you know the great Cherokee warrior, Tsali, left a message with the gold where we found it," Mandie argued. "Remember? He said the gold was for the Cherokees after the white man made peace. In fact, the inscription said it was a curse on the *white* man, not the Indian."

Uncle Ned frowned at her. "Then curse on Jim Shaw's Papoose. And I promise Jim Shaw I watch over Papoose when he go to happy hunting ground."

"My father would not believe in any old curse, Uncle Ned," Mandie assured him. "And neither do I. It's all a bunch of malarkey. God watches over us, remember?"

"Big God not watch over Cherokee when white man take land away," he said, picking up two more bags of nuggets.

Mandie shook her blonde head. "I can't explain that. God sometimes does things that seem bad to us—like taking my father to heaven. But it's to teach us a lesson—how to be better Christians. I don't know what it was, but He must have had a reason for the terrible suffering the Cherokees went through back then." She looked pleadingly at the old man. "Please, Uncle Ned, you believe in God. I know that."

The tall, old Indian set down the bags and hugged the small twelve-year-old. "Papoose right. Must believe in Big God. Now we take gold to Asheville. Build hospital for Cherokees," he relented.

Mandie kissed his dry, withered cheek as he straightened up. Uncle Ned smiled, patted her on the head, and picked up the bags again.

Mandie followed Uncle Ned outside. "And we have to trust God to help us get it there safely," she reminded him.

Tsa'ni, Mandie's Cherokee cousin, sat in the driver's seat of the wagon. "How many more?" he called, "There must be a large amount of gold in there."

Uncle Wirt, Tsa'ni's grandfather, passed a bag to Uncle John at the back door. "You just watch wagon. We load bags," he yelled at Tsa'ni.

Mandie looked startled at the harsh tone of Uncle Wirt's voice. She knew he was still angry with his grandson Tsa'ni for the many bad deeds he had done. But Mandie thought the boy had changed since the time he tried to beat them to the gold. She believed he should be given a chance to prove himself.

Walking to the side of the wagon, Mandie spoke quietly. "There's a little more, Tsa'ni," she told him. "But it's awfully heavy. That's why it's in such small bags. They think it will look more like luggage that way, too."

"Are we taking this gold to the train?" Tsa'ni asked.

"Yes, it's all been kept secret because of the danger involved, but we're going directly from here to the depot. Then we'll take the train to Asheville," Mandie explained in a low voice.

"What happens when we get to Asheville?" Tsa'ni asked.

"We'll put the gold in a bigger bank so it'll be safe. Then we're going to start building the hospital for the Cherokees on some land between Deep Creek and Birdtown," Mandie explained.

"So, it has all been planned," the Indian boy said, "and no one has told me a thing."

Just then Uncle John called to Mandie from the doorway. "Hop in, Mandie. That's all."

Mandie, with Snowball clinging to her shoulder, climbed into the back of the wagon and made a place for herself among the bags of gold. Tsa'ni followed. Uncle John shook hands with Mr. Frady, the banker. "Well, Wilbur, thank you. We've finally got it off your hands," he said.

"Thank goodness!" the short, round man replied. Nervously, he wiped the sweat from his brow. "Maybe I can get some sleep now. That was just a little bit too much for me to worry over, John."

Uncle John turned to the two Indians. "Let's get going," he said. "My wife should be waiting at the depot with the others by now." The three men climbed into the wagon.

"I wish you Godspeed," Mr. Frady called from the doorway.

Uncle John tipped his wide-brimmed hat at Mr. Frady as Uncle Ned shook the reins, and the horses pulled the wagon down the alley past an old drunk and onto the dark, deserted street. It was time for everyone in Bryson City to be at home eating supper.

The train would be in shortly. The whole operation was going smoothly. Their secret seemed well kept.

Snowball nosed around the quilts covering the gold in the bottom of the wagon bed and disappeared underneath in his inspection of the leather bags.

Tsa'ni suddenly made a quick movement and pulled the kitten out from its hiding place, tossing him to Mandie.

"That animal friend of yours knows how to bite," he said, rubbing his leg. Under the quilt his hand touched something. Pulling it out he found an old half-burned candle. He looked at it for a few seconds, then put it in his pocket.

"I'm sorry, Tsa'ni," Mandie apologized. She shook the kitten lightly. "Snowball, you know you aren't supposed to behave like that. Now curl up in my lap and be still," she scolded.

"Where did you get such a cat?" Tsa'ni asked.

"Oh, I've had Snowball since I lived in my father's house at Charley Gap. He goes with me everywhere I go," Mandie said, softly rubbing the kitten's white fur. Snowball purred contentedly. "He's a smart cat. He helped my friends and me escape from the bootleggers who kidnapped us when we got lost in the mountains."

"Now, how did he do that?"

"Well, they tied our hands, and Snowball played with the ends of the rope until it was loose enough for us to get away," Mandie explained. "Snowball also knows when it's time to eat and time to go to bed."

"That is nothing. Most animals know that," Tsa'ni retorted.

A train whistle sounded in the distance and soon the depot came into view.

Uncle John turned around in the front seat. "Remember, Mandie, when we stop, I want you and Tsa'ni to go directly to your mother. She should be right inside. Uncle Ned and Uncle Wirt and I will unload the gold into one of the train cars. We don't want to draw any unnecessary attention."

"Yes, sir, I understand," Mandie answered.

When Uncle Ned stopped the wagon by the depot platform, Mandie stood. "Come on, Tsa'ni. Let's go," she said quietly.

Clutching Snowball, she jumped down. Tsa'ni followed, and they both hurried inside the wooden building where her mother and friends waited.

When Elizabeth, Mandie's mother, saw the two through the doorway, she stood up from the long bench where she and the other young people were sitting.

Mandie looked around the large room. *This place looks like a church with all these benches like pews,* she thought. There was even a wood stove standing in the middle of the floor, just like the one in their church back home in Franklin.

Elizabeth met her daughter with a hug. "I already have all the tickets, so we can get right on the train," she said as the train came puffing up and stopped by the platform.

"Sallie, Joe, Dimar, get your things. Here are yours, Amanda." She gave Mandie a small bag. They were only carrying the essentials for overnight because they planned to go home to Franklin from Asheville.

Together they boarded the first passenger car and sat down to wait for the men.

Since Mandie had been on a train only once before, her excitement was hard to contain. She wanted to see and feel everything. Sitting on a long cross seat at the end of the car and beside the other young people, she rubbed the soft, dark upholstery and looked around in the dim lamplight. There were only a few other passengers.

Sallie, Uncle Ned's granddaughter, straightened her long, dark dress, which had been made especially for this journey. "I have never been to Asheville," she said. "I am excited about going there." She pulled her bright red shawl around her shoulders.

"I've been to Asheville several times with my father," said Joe, Dr. Woodard's son. "It's a beautiful town but it's full of hills. And, boy, does it get cold at night in that place."

"I look forward to seeing the great home of Mr. Vanderbilt," said Dimar, the Cherokee boy who was with them when they found the gold.

"Oh, Dimar," Mandie laughed, as she rubbed Snowball's fur. "We aren't going to visit Mr. Vanderbilt. Are we, Mother?"

Elizabeth smiled at the conversation and said, "I doubt it, but I do know the man."

Mandie sat up straight and the others leaned forward. "Really, Mother?" Mandie asked.

"Well, actually, my father knew him," her mother replied. "Don't forget that I lived in Asheville a long time before I married your Uncle John."

"Why, yes, I hadn't thought of that," Mandie said. She turned to Dimar. "I don't know whether you understand or not, Dimar," she said. "You see, my grandmother had my mother's marriage to my father annulled when I was born."

Dimar looked puzzled but continued to listen. "She told Mother I had died. Then Grandmother gave me to my father and told him that my mother didn't ever want to see him again. So he took me and moved to Swain County where he married another woman. I always thought *she* was my mother until my father died and I found my Uncle John in Franklin. He's my father's brother. Uncle John knew where my real mother was in Asheville, and he asked her and my grandmother to come to his house so we could see each other. Then my mother and Uncle John got married. See?" She took a deep breath.

Elizabeth smiled at Mandie's long explanation.

"I knew some of that by listening," Dimar said. "That is interesting, like a storybook. Are we going to visit your grandmother in Asheville?"

Mandie turned to her mother for an answer. She knew her grandmother didn't like the fact that Uncle John had exposed her long-kept secret. And she wasn't very happy that Elizabeth had married John. "Are we, Mother?" Mandie asked.

"My mother is away visiting relatives in Charleston, and I'm not sure what your Uncle John has planned for us," Elizabeth told her.

Just then Uncle John came up the aisle with Uncle Wirt right behind him. "I've made plans for us to stay at the hotel," he said, sitting beside his wife.

"A hotel? What is a hotel?" Mandie asked.

The other youngsters were wide-eyed with interest. In 1900 few young people in western North Carolina had traveled very far from home.

Sallie and Dimar waited for an explanation, too. With a knowing grin, Joe crossed his arms and leaned back in his seat.

"A hotel is a place where you pay to spend the night," Uncle John explained. "It has bedrooms to sleep in that they rent out by the night and a dining room where you can buy your meals. It's for travelers."

Sallie looked confused. "We are going to buy a bedroom to sleep in?"

Joe laughed. "No, silly, you don't buy a bedroom. You only pay so much money per night to be allowed to sleep in the room."

"And how do you happen to know so much about it, Mister Doctor's Son?" Mandie asked, sarcastically.

Joe straightened his shoulders. "Because I *am* a doctor's son," he said, "and a doctor travels a lot. I have often stayed in a hotel with my father when he allowed me to travel with him."

"You have?" Dimar asked.

"Sure," Joe said. "But it's not that exciting. It's just a room with a bed in it. You just go in the room and go to sleep like you do at home, only the hotel rooms are real fancy, and there are lots and lots of bedrooms in one big building. And there are all kinds of people sleeping in the same building." Joe enjoyed being the center of attention. "When you're hungry," he explained, "you go into this huge room with lots of tables and you tell the lady what you want to eat, and she brings you the food. That's all there is to it, except you have to pay money for it."

Uncle John smiled. "You sound like a well-seasoned traveler, Joe."

Mandie frowned. "Well, who sleeps in the same room with you?" she asked.

"No one, silly, unless you want them to." Joe laughed. "When you pay money for the room, you tell them who is to sleep in the room. That's all." he explained.

"Then we are all going to sleep in one room?" Sallie asked.

"No, Sallie," Uncle John told her. "You see, each room has only one big bed, so we will need at least four rooms—one for you and Mandie, one for Uncle Wirt and Uncle Ned, another for Mandie's mother and me, and we'll see if all three of the boys can manage in one room."

Sallie was shocked. "Oh, but that is so many rooms, and you have to pay money for each room. Could we not all sleep in one room? It would not cost so much money that way," the Indian girl reasoned.

"That's not the way hotels do business, Sallie," Uncle John replied. "Usually only two people can sleep in a room. But don't worry about the money. It has all been taken care of."

"It sounds like fun, Sallie." Mandie giggled. "You and I get a whole room all by ourselves."

"You must promise not to talk all night, though," Elizabeth cautioned them.

"Uncle John"—Mandie changed the subject—"where is Uncle Ned?"

"He stayed with the cargo back in the baggage car," Uncle John said in a low voice. "After a while Uncle Wirt and I will take our turns looking after it. We thought it would be better if we didn't let it completely out of our sight."

The train gave a lurch and the couplings between the cars clanged as it began pulling out of the station. The sudden movement caught the young people unaware and they fell against each other, laughing.

"Away we go!" shouted Mandie above the noise.

The whistle blew, and the train picked up speed as it rounded the bend, leaving town and safety behind. None of them knew what danger lurked ahead in the dark night.

Chapter 2 / Ghost Bandits in the Dark

After a while the journey became monotonous. In the dark there was nothing to look at through the windows, and the train crept slowly around the mountain.

Bored, Mandie came up with an idea. "Why don't we go back and see Uncle Ned for a little while?" she suggested. "He's all alone back there. Want to?"

"Yes!" cried her equally bored friends.

"Could we, Mother?" Mandie asked.

Elizabeth looked at John. "What do you think?"

"Well, I suppose it'd be all right," John answered. "Just don't stay too long," he told them. "And Sallie, tell your grandfather I'll be back in a little while to relieve him."

"Yes, sir," Sallie replied, as they stood up and started down the aisle of the train car.

"And please be careful when you go from one car to the other," Elizabeth called. "It could be dangerous if you don't watch your step."

"We will," they promised as they went out the door at the end of the car. When they stepped onto the platform between the cars, the cold mountain wind whipped around them and the noise of the train was deafening. They hurried into the next car.

Joe quickly shut the door behind them and stood there shivering for a moment. "I thought it was supposed to be summertime," he laughed.

"Yes, but the wind is always cold at night in the mountains," Dimar told him.

"A breath of cold air is good for us," Tsa'ni added.

There were a few passengers in the car they had just entered, but when they moved to the next car they found it completely empty.

Sallie looked around the dimly-lit car. "There certainly aren't many people on this train," she remarked.

Mandie stopped to look out a window. She leaned against the glass. "Look!" she cried, pointing outside. "Horsemen!"

The group crowded in front of the window.

"In the moonlight they look like ghosts," Mandie joked.

Joe cupped his hand against the window to see better. "What are they wearing over their clothes?" he asked.

"I do not know, but they are keeping pace with the train," Tsa'ni answered.

"It is too dark to see their faces," Dimar said.

"Oh, they see us!" Mandie said, waving her hand.

Joe looked away from the window. "I think they're trying to get on the train," he warned.

Suddenly, the train jerked to a stop. All five young people staggered and grabbed for anything to keep from falling. The train had stopped on a hill, and they found it difficult to stand upright. They all looked at each other questioningly.

"Why are we stopping here?" Sallie asked.

"I don't know," Joe answered, "but something is wrong."

Just then, a loud clang came from the direction of

the baggage car. Dimar led the way as they rushed to the back door of the car to see what had happened. Dimar tried to open the door. It was stuck. He peered out the window. "The baggage car," he cried. "It has come apart from the rest of the train! It is rolling back down the track!"

"Oh, no!" Mandie yelled. "Uncle Ned . . ."

"Grandfather!" Sallie screamed.

Joe pushed his way to the window to look. At that moment there was a deafening crash. He turned slowly. Both girls were in tears, and a sick look of realization covered the faces of Dimar and Tsa'ni.

Mandie ran for the front door of the train car and threw it open. Joe hurried after her and the others followed.

Outside, Mandie hopped off the train and blindly started in the direction of the baggage car. Snowball clung to her shoulder in fright. Joe and the others stepped off the train more cautiously.

"Mandie! Wait!" Joe called. "Look! We're right on the edge of a steep ridge."

Mandie stopped. In the dim moonlight she could see the sharp drop-off just a few feet away. Her heart thumped louder as she realized the danger she was in.

Joe rushed to her side and took her hand. "Come on, all of you," he commanded. "Let's get back to the others on the train. We can't find that baggage car by ourselves."

But just as they turned to get back on, there was a loud noise and the train started up again.

They all froze in panic. By the time they could think clearly enough to run, it was too late. The train was going too fast and all five of them could never get on board without someone getting hurt.

Mandie hid her face in her hands and cried.

Sallie began to shake all over. "Grandfather!" she

wailed. "Now, how will we get help for my grandfather?"

Tsa'ni put his arm around her shoulders. "Do not cry, Sallie. We will, somehow," he said.

Sallie pulled away and bumped into Dimar. Dimar grabbed her arm to keep her from falling.

"Do not move. It is steep here," Dimar told her.

"Doo-oo not moo-oove at a-a-all-ll," said a spooky voice behind them.

The young people whirled to see one of the horsemen seemingly float toward them. As he drew nearer they could see he was wearing a flowing, ground-length, light-colored cape and a light wide-brimmed hat. A tiger mask covered his face, and he carried a dimly-lit lantern. He looked huge.

The young people stood speechless with fright. They huddled together as he approached.

The ghostly man swung the lantern up to light their faces and spoke in an angry, eerie voice. "Wha-a-at are you-oo do-oo-inng he-e-ere?" he asked.

Dimar, with a protective arm around Sallie, looked him boldly in the face. "We were on the train when the baggage car wrecked," he answered. "And when we came out to see what happened, the train pulled away. But who are you and what do you want?" Dimar asked.

The creature spat tobacco juice on the ground and held the lantern closer to Dimar's face. "We-ell-ll-ll, what da ya kn-now-w, ah In-n-n-ju-u-un!" he taunted in his spooky voice. He swung the lantern in front of the other faces. "Thr-ree-ee In-n-ju-u-uns! Well-ll now-ow, wha-a-at air you-oo two-oo whi-i-ite young-un-ns do-oo-in-n' with the-e-ese hyar In-n-ju-u-uns?"

Mandie stepped forward, angry about the insinuation. "The three Indians happen to be our friends. Not only that, I am one-fourth Cherokee myself," she retorted, flipping her blonde hair.

At Mandie's sudden movement, Snowball dug his claws into her shoulder. Mandie winced and took the kitten into her arms.

"Too-oo ba-a-ad you-oo got offuh that trai-ain-n."

Just then, two other ghostlike figures materialized out of the darkness. They were both dressed exactly like the first.

One of them cleared his throat. "Watcha got hyar?" he asked. "By grannies, we're agonna hafta do sumpumm with these hyar younguns."

The third creature pulled a rope from under his long, flowing costume. "Better tie their hands behind 'em, and git 'em on the wagon and take 'em so fur away they cain't innerfear."

He grabbed Dimar's hands and tied them behind him as the first creature tied Tsa'ni's and Joe's. The other one tied the girls' hands behind them. Afraid to fight back or run away, the young people shivered on the edge of the mountain in the semi-darkness. They had no idea whether or not the men were armed.

The first creature spoke again, dropping his spooky voice disguise. "Tiger number two, you and Tiger number three take 'em away. I'll git back to work. Hurry up and git goin'."

Joe spoke up. "Mister, if you'll just let us go, we'll find our way home and won't bother you."

"No, we won't bother you," Mandie agreed. "We only want to find my family and Sallie's grandfather. Whatever your work is, we won't interfere."

"I say you won't innerfear," the first creature replied. "Git goin'."

He disappeared into the darkness. The second creature motioned with his lantern for the young people to follow him. The third creature brought up the rear.

Silently, they walked single file along the railroad track for a few yards. Then Mandie stopped suddenly, turned her face to the sky, and spoke, "What time we are afraid," she paused and Joe joined her in the last part, "we will put our trust in thee, dear God," they said.

The creature bringing up the rear overheard them and gave Joe a shove.

"Git a move on!" he muttered. "Ain't no God up thar gonna hyar you."

"Oh, but God does hear us, and He does answer our prayers," Mandie insisted.

The creature leading the way walked back to "take care of" Mandie when Joe stepped between them.

"You leave her alone, mister," Joe demanded.

"Well, then, you'd better tell her to shet up. And keep yourself quiet, too," the creature replied. "Else all of ya gonna git whut's comin' to ya."

Mandie whispered in Joe's ear. "Sorry. I'll be quiet, but I'll still pray."

Joe smiled at her.

"Up this trail! Git!" the creature ordered as he led the way.

The group stumbled silently among the brush and rocks as they climbed the mountainside. They stayed close to one another, having no idea what their fate would be, and worried about what had happened to the others.

After a short time they came to what looked like an old wagon trail. There, all alone, stood an old wagon with two horses hitched to it.

"In the wagon!" yelled the creature leading them.

The young people looked at one another silently. With their hands still tied, they managed to climb into the back of the wagon. The two creatures sat on the seat—one sitting backwards to watch them; the other, whipping the horses into a run. The trail was terribly rough. The wagon lurched over rocks and bumps and holes in the darkness, jostling the youngsters from side to side.

Snowball, still clinging to Mandie, protested loudly. Mandie tried her best to hold onto him by turning her head sidewise and raising her shoulder.

The wagon finally came to a halt in front of a deserted hut with a low, steeply-slanted roof. In the woods, Mandie had lost all sense of direction and wondered how they would ever find their way back.

The driver stepped down from the wagon. "Out and inside!" he ordered.

They could do nothing but obey. Inside the dark hut the first creature swung his lantern around, inspecting the interior. The other one stayed outside. The dim light showed no windows and only one door. The hut was just one big room with a huge rock fireplace. The young people looked around in dismay, afraid to speak. A nearby shelf held an old coffeepot, tin plates, and utensils. A pile of dirty, ragged quilts lay in one corner on the floor. That was all they could see.

The creature turned to go. "Now we're gonna put an iron padlock and chains on the door outside so thar ain't no way ya kin git out of hyar, and thar ain't no use yer tryin'," he sneered. "That'll teach ya to poke into other people's business."

"Please, mister, if you'd just let us go, we'll go straight home," Mandie begged.

"Yeh, go home by way of the wrecked train to see

what happened to thet gold, eh? Ain't no way we gonna let ya go. We gonna git thet gold and be gone 'fore ya ever git out of hyar, *if ever.*" He gave an evil laugh. "Ya may never git out of hyar. This is a deserted part of the mountains. Ain't no one ever comes this way. So we done got y'all tuck care of." He laughed again, stepped outside, and closed the heavy log door.

With the sound of a metal padlock and chains fastening on the outside, Mandie and her friends became prisoners with little hope of ever being rescued.

Chapter 3 / The Little Bird

With the lantern gone, the hut became dark as pitch. The group huddled together in the center of the floor and helped one another untie their hands.

"If we only had a light," Sallie wished out loud.

With that reminder, Tsa'ni thrust his hands into his pockets and triumphantly produced the candle he had found in Uncle Ned's wagon. "Wish granted," he said smartly, although no one could see what he had. He stood up and felt his way to the huge fireplace on the back wall.

Sallie heard him moving about. "What do you mean?" she asked.

"Tsa'ni, where are you going?" Joe stood up, trying to find him.

"I am going to make a light for Sallie," the Indian boy said from near the fireplace. "If I can only find something to strike a flame."

"Are you going to build a fire in the fireplace?" Dimar asked.

"No. It might smoke and suffocate us because there is no ventilation in here," Tsa'ni replied.

The others could hear him striking stones. Suddenly

a spark caught a piece of straw in the fireplace and flamed. They gathered around him and then saw the candle in his hand.

"Where did you get the candle?" Dimar asked.

"That's the candle you found in Uncle Ned's wagon!" Mandie cried. "He found it in the wagon after we loaded the gold at the bank," she explained.

"Yes," Tsa'ni said. He lit the candle, stomped on the burning straw, and set the candle in one of the tin plates on the hearth. "See what I did for you, Sallie?"

"Thank you, Tsa'ni," Sallie answered gratefully.

The flame threw a dim light around the room. They all gathered near the candle and sat down once more. Snowball curled up on Mandie's lap for a nap.

Sallie sighed. "Oh, my poor grandfather!" she said sorrowfully. "I wonder where he is!"

"And I wish I knew where my mother and Uncle John are right now," Mandie added. "How did all this happen, anyway?"

"Somehow those ghost creatures must have known about the gold on the train and caused the wreck," Dimar mused.

"I'm sure your folks are all right, Mandie," Joe comforted. "Don't worry."

There was a long silence. Tears came into Sallie's eyes as she envisioned her grandfather at the bottom of the ravine.

Mandie reached over to take Sallie's dark hand in her own small white one. "We have to trust God to take care of all of them, Sallie," Mandie said, "and figure out a way to get us out of this place." She glanced around the cabin, hoping to find some way to escape.

Snowball stirred and jumped out of Mandie's lap.

Prowling around the cabin, he uncovered an old rope among the dirty quilts and played with it, scooting the end across the floor.

"Look what Snowball found!" Mandie cried.

"What good is a rope to us?" Joe asked.

"Maybe we could think of some plan to use the rope to escape," Dimar suggested. "Let us all try."

The young people grew silent again, trying to think of possible uses for the rope. Suddenly there was a twittering noise and a small bird flew down from the rafters. Snowball, at once alert, began chasing it.

"A bird! Snowball, come back here and leave that little bird alone!" Mandie scolded.

But Snowball had other plans. He chased the bewildered little bird around the room until it finally beat its wings against the huge fireplace and found the chimney opening. The bird disappeared. Mandie tried to grab the kitten, but she was a few seconds too late. Hungry for the little bird, Snowball clawed his way right up the inside chimney wall.

Mandie stood at the fireplace trying to see up the chimney. Soon the scratching noises stopped, and the frightened meowing began.

"Snowball! Come back down here, you silly cat!" Mandie called. "Kitty, kitty! Snowball!"

"He must have thought the chimney was a tree!" Joe laughed.

Mandie cocked her head in an effort to see where the kitten was. "Joe, it's not funny! How in the world will I ever be able to get him down?" Mandie wailed.

Dimar came and stood beside her. "I will go up and get him!" he offered.

"Go up the chimney?" Sallie frowned.

"Yes, it is quite wide. I think I can manage," Dimar insisted. "Snowball must be holding onto the rocks inside the chimney." Dimar stooped to pick up the candle and tried to shine the light up the chimney.

"I think he has gone too far up, Dimar. You can't reach him," Mandie moaned, clenching her fists.

"Dimar can climb the chimney," Tsa'ni said. "I know how, too."

"Climb the chimney?" Mandie questioned. "Dimar, you might fall!"

"I will not fall," Dimar told her. "You see, by bracing my toes on one side of the chimney and my backside on the other, I can push myself up and reach Snowball. I will not fall."

"If you can do that," Mandie reasoned, "maybe we could all climb the chimney and get out of here.—What do you think, Sallie?"

"I think we should try it," the Indian girl agreed.

Mandie picked up the rope Snowball had been playing with. "What if we tied the rope up on the roof like we did in the cave when we rescued Tsa'ni from that pit?" she asked.

Tsa'ni examined the rope. "It might work if the rope is long enough," he said.

Joe grabbed one end and stretched the rope across the room. "It's a lot longer than this room is wide," he said.

Dimar took the rope from Joe. "Yes, it looks long enough," he said. "I will take the rope with me and climb all the way to the top. After I secure it there, I will throw the end back down the chimney for you to use in climbing," he told them.

The others anxiously watched as Dimar, with the rope

coiled around his shoulder, disappeared into the black recesses of the chimney.

Snowball continued to meow for help.

"Let us know when you find Snowball *and* when you get to the top, please!" Mandie called.

After a few moments Dimar yelled down to them. "I now have Snowball on my shoulder," he said.

"Oh, thank you!" Mandie said gratefully.

They all waited around the fireplace in silence. Then there was a loud clattering noise, and the girls cried out in fear.

"Dimar! What was that?" Joe called up the chimney.

"It is just me on the roof. It is made of tin." Dimar's voice came faintly down the chimney. "I have Snowball out, too. I am fastening the rope around the top of the chimney and will throw the end down to you. Here it comes!"

There was a swishing sound and the end of the rope appeared in the dim candlelight in the fireplace. Joe lunged forward and grabbed it.

"We have it, Dimar," he called. He turned to the others. "Girls first. Sallie or Mandie?"

"Sallie, you go first," Mandie told her Indian friend.

"All right, but, Mandie, please be careful when you come up. It looks rather frightening," Sallie told her. She took the end of the rope, stooped to put her head up the chimney, and then stood up. Grasping the rope tightly, she swung herself off the stone floor. As her feet touched the side of the chimney she kept moving her hands up the rope. The rope was rough and her hands burned as she climbed. Her arms felt as though they were going to pull out of their sockets, but with determination she made her way up.

At the top Dimar helped Sallie climb out of the chimney onto the steep, tin roof. Her legs trembled as she stood, but she breathed a sigh of relief. She smelled the soot on her skin and clothes and tried to brush it off with her hands. "I made it, Dimar, but I must be rather dirty," she said.

Dimar laughed. "It does not matter. We will all be dirty," the Indian boy said. Leaning over the top of the chimney, he called, "Who is next?"

Stooping carefully on the slick roof, Sallie picked up Mandie's kitten from where he sat licking himself. "Snowball doesn't like the dirt either," she said.

Inside the hut, Mandie grasped the end of the rope and worked her way up the chimney as Sallie had done. Soot, loosened by the rubbing of the rope, fell into her face and hair, and she squinted to keep it out of her eyes. Suddenly, she felt her skirt catch on something. She tried to wriggle free, but it tore. *Mother will—* She stopped mid-thought. *Mother will be glad I'm alive*, she decided, *if I ever get out of this chimney*.

When she finally got to the top, Mandie felt Dimar's strong hands lift her out of the chimney and onto the roof next to Sallie.

"Do not move!" Sallie warned, handing the kitten to Mandie. "The roof is very steep."

Mandie tried to stand still as she smoothed Snowball's dirty, white fur.

Dimar called for one of the boys to come up.

Joe offered the rope to Tsa'ni. "You go next."

"I will wait. I must put out the candle before I leave," Tsa'ni replied. "I will go after you."

"Well, if you insist," Joe said, grasping the end of the rope.

When Joe arrived safely at the top, Dimar called for Tsa'ni.

Tsa'ni blew out the candle, rolled it in some old ashes for it to cool, and then put it in his pocket. Taking hold of the rope, he pushed himself up and began the climb easily. Suddenly, about halfway up, he felt something give.

"The rope is about to break!" he called to the others on the roof.

Mandie bit her lip. "Please, dear God, don't let it break now!" she cried.

Dimar called down to him, "Try to hurry. Maybe you can get up before it breaks."

But it was too late. At that moment the rope snapped. Tsa'ni braced his feet against one wall and his backside against the wall behind him. He was going to have to work his way up without the rope. It was a miracle he hadn't fallen.

The young people waited fearfully on the roof. Hearing nothing more, Dimar leaned over the top of the chimney. "Tsa'ni, are you all right?" he called.

"Yes, I am all right," Tsa'ni answered. "The rope broke, but I can work my way up."

They could hear the scuffling noise as the Indian boy moved on up the chimney.

Dimar pulled on the remaining piece of rope. Excited, he called down to Tsa'ni. "There is quite a long piece of rope left. If you can manage to get far enough to reach it, you can use it the rest of the way," he said as he tossed it back down the chimney.

"I will try," Tsa'ni replied.

"Poor Tsa'ni. He is always getting into trouble," Mandie moaned.

"Usually through his own doings, though," Joe added.

"But this is not his fault," Sallie defended him.

"I guess not. In fact, it could have been me on the broken rope. He wanted to be last so he could put out the candle and bring it with him," Joe explained.

Just then Tsa'ni called from inside the chimney. "I have the rope!" he said.

Dimar checked to see that it was secure. "It seems to be all right at this end," he answered.

In a few moments a scratched and bruised Tsa'ni appeared at the top of the chimney. He, too, was covered with soot. Dimar and Joe helped him out onto the tin roof.

"Good exercise!" Tsa'ni laughed, rubbing his scratched back.

"Now all we have to do is slide down this roof and jump to the ground," Dimar told them. "Thank goodness the cabin has a low roof. It will not be so far to jump."

"Sounds like fun when we can't see what we're jumping into," Joe laughed.

"I will go first and see what is beneath," Dimar told them. "Listen for me. I will look all the way around the cabin and pick the best side for you to jump."

"I do not mind going first," Tsa'ni offered.

"Neither do I," Joe chimed in.

"No, you two stay with the girls and help them slide down when I call to you," Dimar said, lying down on his stomach. Pushing himself off with his hands, he started sliding down backwards. It was too dark to see much, but the others heard the thud when Dimar landed on the ground.

"I am down!" Dimar yelled.

He walked all around the cabin. "I think the best place

is where I came down. There is more grass and weeds here. Not so many thorny bushes."

"All right, we'll send Sallie first," Joe called to Dimar.

Sallie looked at the steep roof and took a deep breath. Twisting her heavy skirt around her, she lay on her stomach and gave herself a backward push as she had seen Dimar do. Before she could plop onto the ground, Dimar broke her fall.

"Mandie coming next," Joe called to Dimar.

"What will I do with Snowball?" Mandie protested. "How will I get him down?"

"Here," said Tsa'ni, pulling the rope off the chimney. "We will tie this around him and you hold onto the end of the rope as you slide down. He will have to come with you whether he likes it or not."

"It won't hurt him?"

"No, it will not hurt him," Tsa'ni replied. "Hold him still while I roll this rope around him."

Snowball did not like the idea, but Tsa'ni rolled the rope around and around the kitten until he couldn't get loose. He gave the end of the rope to Mandie.

"Snowball, be still!" Mandie ordered. "We have to slide down to the ground." She rubbed his head, and he purred. But he would not be still.

Lying down on the roof as she had seen Sallie do, she grasped the rope and slid down, pulling the protesting kitten with her. Sallie caught him as he came off the roof and Dimar broke the fall for Mandie.

Mandie took the howling kitten in her arms and untied the rope. "You shouldn't carry on so, Snowball. Remember, this was all your idea," she told him as she stroked his ruffled fur. He was soon purring softly.

Tsa'ni came down next, with Joe following.

At last the young people, grimy with soot, were safely on the ground outside the cabin. They stood close together in the dark.

"Now what do we do?" Sallie asked.

"We have to find everybody, so we'll just start walking, I guess," Mandie replied.

"But my grandfather is probably in one direction and your mother and the others in the opposite direction. Remember?" Sallie said, trying to brush more of the dirt from her dress.

"I think we should find our way back to the wrecked train," Dimar suggested. "When your mother and Uncle John and Tsa'ni's grandfather can get off the train, I think they would head back toward the wreck to find us."

"Yes, you're right, Dimar," Joe agreed, adjusting the suspenders on his trousers. "That sounds sensible."

"I know my grandfather would come back to find us," Tsa'ni said.

"And *my* grandfather may still be in that wrecked baggage car!" Sallie cried.

Poor Uncle Ned, Mandie thought, *he may have been killed when the baggage car wrecked. Please, God, let him be all right.*

"Then it is agreed. We will try to find our way back to where the train wrecked," Dimar said.

"Yes," the others answered.

"I will walk in front," Dimar declared, "and Tsa'ni, you and Joe walk behind the girls. That way they will be protected." He turned to go.

"Protected?" Mandie asked shakily.

"Yes, from anyone or any *thing* we might meet on our way," Dimar explained.

Mandie shivered as she remembered the panther she

had encountered on her first visit to her Cherokee kin-people. "Thank you, Dimar," she replied and took Sallie's hand. Her other hand clutched Snowball to her shoulder.

So the group went down the vague trail with only a little moonlight to illumine their way. Worry showed on their faces as they hastened their steps to find the others. They didn't know what they would find, but they had to get back to the wrecked train car.

Chapter 4 / Runaway Train

When the train stopped, the adults heard the noise of the wrecked car but didn't know what was happening. Then the train started up again and began picking up speed. Uncle John went back to look for the young people and found the baggage car missing and no sign of Mandie and her friends. The other passengers were frightened, too. They said they had seen the youngsters go on into the next car but they hadn't returned.

Terror gripped Elizabeth. She didn't know whether Mandie and Uncle Ned and the other youngsters had been in the wrecked car or not. Uncle Wirt and Uncle John tried to comfort her, but the engine was going so fast around the curves it was all they could do to stay on their seats. The train was so noisy they couldn't even talk.

Elizabeth practically screamed in her husband's ear. "John, we've got to get off this train and go back to see what happened to Amanda, and Uncle Ned, and the other children!" she cried.

John, with his arm tightly around her, nodded his head in agreement. He was too worried to talk.

Uncle Wirt sat opposite them with a furious expression on his old face. He, too, was worried.

The train came to a sudden, screeching halt and almost threw them to the floor. They looked out the windows. It was so dark outside they couldn't see a thing. Everything became still. Everyone was waiting to see what was going to happen next. There was the sound of a horse galloping away into the distance.

The engineer opened the door at the end of the car and came inside. "I am very sorry, ladies and gentlemen," he began, as he wiped the sweat from his round, red face. "A bandit left his horse and climbed on board when they stopped the train a ways back, and he forced me to open up, full-throttle. Then, a little while ago, he jumped off."

"Why?" Elizabeth managed to ask, shakily.

"I don't rightly know, ma'am," he replied. "You see, they uncoupled the baggage car when they stopped the train back yonder and it went down into the gorge—"

"—Amanda, Uncle Ned, the children!" Elizabeth cried, unable to stop shaking.

John held her tightly against him. "Is that the only car that went off the track?" he asked the man.

"Yes, sir, far as I could tell in the dark," the engineer replied.

"Maybe the children got off when the train stopped," John suggested. "You know how curious and adventuresome they are."

Uncle Wirt clasped his hands together. "But we not sure, and Ned in baggage car, and baggage car in gorge for sure," he reminded them.

"I'm afraid he was. But maybe he managed to get out," John said, grasping for hope.

"What are we going to do?" Elizabeth asked the engineer.

"We're almost in Asheville, so we'll go into the station," the man replied. "If you'll all be patient, I'll go back up front and get this train—what's left of it—into the depot."

He turned and went back out the door.

"We must remember not to mention the gold to anyone," Uncle John cautioned Elizabeth and Uncle Wirt.

"Of course, John," Elizabeth replied, still in tears. "If this train can't go back, how are we going to get back to where the car went off the track?"

John still tried to comfort her. "We'll get some horses in Asheville and head toward Franklin. From there we'll go up the mountain. It's too steep and dangerous to ride back in from Asheville. Besides, I'm hoping the youngsters and Uncle Ned will head for our house in Franklin if they are able to."

Uncle Wirt leaned forward. "We get help, find lost ones. Find bad men, too," he told Elizabeth.

She managed a weak smile through her tears and put her hand over the old man's. "Thank you, Uncle Wirt," she said.

The train slowed as it came into Asheville. John, Elizabeth and Uncle Wirt picked up their belongings and prepared to leave the train.

There was no one around except the baggage boy and the stationmaster. When the stationmaster heard what had happened, he was very upset. "There won't be another train going back that direction until tomorrow," he said.

John asked him about the local livery stables. "We

need a light wagon or buggy to take up to Franklin," he said.

Elizabeth interrupted, "No, John, get three horses. You know I can ride astride as well as anyone. It'll be much faster."

"The trip will be awfully rough for you," John warned.

"Don't worry about that," she said. "All I want right now is speed. We must hurry."

"All right, if you say so." John disappeared with the baggage boy and soon returned with three horses from the livery stables.

Uncle Wirt led the way through shortcuts he knew in the woods. Some of the trails were so overgrown they didn't look like trails anymore, but the old Indian knew every step of the way.

Well into the morning they arrived in Franklin. Tired and dirty, they tethered the horses in front of the house. John helped Elizabeth dismount.

Jason Bond, the caretaker, came to the front door when they rode up. He couldn't believe what he was seeing. They were supposed to be in Asheville. "Mr. Shaw, what has happened?" he inquired, hurrying down the walkway.

While John explained, Elizabeth stood by the horses, trying to adjust her heavy skirts that had become twisted and wrinkled during the hard ride. She was a little shaky, but proud to have kept up with the men.

"We only need a bite to eat, Jason, and fresh horses and we'll be off," John told him, as they all walked to the front porch.

"Let me get a horse and go with you, Mr. Shaw," Jason begged.

"No, Jason, we need you here in case they come home," John told him. "Uncle Wirt and I will go."

Elizabeth stopped and touched John's arm. "You aren't going anywhere without me," she said.

"But there's nothing you can do. You're all worn out, darling. Let Uncle Wirt and me take care of things," John replied.

"Absolutely not! I am going with you!" Elizabeth was adamant.

"Dr. Woodard, Joe's father, is in town," Jason said. "He came by last night. Said he wouldn't go back home until tomorrow. He'll probably want to go with you."

"If he's not here on a life-and-death case, I hope he *can* go with us. We might need a doctor," John told him. "While we're eating, see if you can find him, or get word to him to come over at once."

Aunt Lou, the housekeeper, heard the commotion and was waiting for them at the front door. Elizabeth told her the news, and the large black woman wiped tears from her round cheeks with her apron.

"Lawsy mercy, my chile, she done got lost!" Aunt Lou cried, "and all them other 'lil ones, and that pore old Mister Ned." She put her arm around Elizabeth. "And Miz 'Lizbeth, you looks like you gonna drop any minute."

"I'll be fine as soon as I eat," Elizabeth told her. "I'll run upstairs and change into some riding clothes. You get Jenny to set out some food for us."

Uncle Wirt stood silently at the door. He, like the others, was worried about what they might find when they got back to the wrecked train car.

A short time later, while they were hastily eating, Liza ushered Dr. Woodard into the dining room. "Well, John, what brings you back so soon? I thought you all were going on to Asheville," he said.

John rose to pull out a chair at the table. "Sit down,

sit down," he invited. "Liza, bring Dr. Woodard a plate."

As they informed Dr. Woodard of the situation, he assured them that he would go with them. His son, Joe, was among those who discovered the gold. Dr. Woodard was the only other person who knew about the transfer.

Within minutes the four adults left on horseback. They were well equipped with extra blankets, ropes, lanterns, and food, and Uncle Wirt guided them through the trails he knew.

Some time later they came upon an old cabin by a stream in the woods. Uncle Wirt slowed his horse to dismount. "I send word to Bird-town," he said.

"That's a good idea, Uncle Wirt, and Deep Creek, too," John suggested.

A young Indian man who evidently knew Uncle Wirt came from behind the house. They exchanged Cherokee greetings, and Uncle Wirt explained where they were going.

"You go Deep Creek and Bird-town. Need braves at train," the old man ordered.

"I go like lightning," the young man replied. Instantly he ran to the pony tied by the side of the house and was on his way.

"Braves find bad men," Uncle Wirt told his three companions.

All four were silent as they traveled on. What would they find when they got to the wrecked train?

Chapter 5 / Tsa'ni in Trouble

"Won't we ever get there?" Joe complained, as he stumbled over the exposed root of a huge tree in the darkness.

"The railroad track is not very far now." Dimar spoke from the front of the group. "When we find it, we will walk down the tracks until we come to the place where the train wrecked."

"Dimar, are you serious?" Mandie asked. "You know part of the track is high up in the air. We could fall off in the dark."

"We will hold hands. Then if one slips, the others can keep him from falling," Dimar explained as they continued through the woods.

"But if we hold hands we will have to walk sideways," Sallie informed him.

Tsa'ni spoke up. "I still have the piece of rope," he said. "We could hold onto the rope together."

"Hey! Remember that time we got lost in the mountains and those bootleggers tied us up? We could tie all of us together the way they did," Joe suggested.

"That sounds like a good way to do it," Sallie agreed.

She held her dark, full skirt above her ankles in an effort to avoid the briars in the underbrush.

"Yes, that's the best idea yet," Mandie said, holding tightly to her kitten.

"Well, we must begin using the rope then, because there is the railroad track. Up the hill there," Dimar told them, motioning in the darkness.

"I can't see a thing," Mandie said.

"Neither can I," Joe added.

"Dimar, how do you see that far?" Sallie asked.

"Now I see the tracks," Mandie said, excitedly.

"Yes, they were there all the time," Tsa'ni said sarcastically.

When the young people reached the tracks, as Joe had suggested, they began working with the rope. Dimar fastened one end around his waist and gave the free end to Sallie. She, in turn, wrapped it around her waist and passed it on to Mandie, who did likewise, then Joe, and then Tsa'ni.

"It is just barely long enough," Tsa'ni said, securing the rope around his waist. "Now if one falls, we all fall."

"Oh, no, Tsa'ni," Mandie disagreed. "You see, there would be four of us left standing to pull the other one back up."

"Then we had better be quick if one of us falls," Tsa'ni replied.

Dimar carefully stepped onto the tracks and the others lined up behind him. But before Dimar could give the word to start, Mandie spoke up.

"I think we should ask God to protect us," she said. "I'm scared."

"The rope will protect us," Tsa'ni retorted.

"Tsa'ni!" Sallie rebuked. "Of course the rope will help

us, but we need God to watch over us."

"I do not believe in the white people's God," Tsa'ni said vehemently.

Dimar was shocked. "But you go to church with your father and your grandfather," he said.

"Yes, but that is only because they make me go. When I am grown I will not go to church anymore. They will not be able to force me," Tsa'ni answered.

Mandie's heart cried out in pain. *Tsa'ni did not believe in God!* What could she say to him to convince him he was wrong? She knew he was quite stubborn and sometimes quite mean, so she would have to be very careful with whatever she said.

"Tsa'ni, just say our little verse with us. We always say it to God when we're afraid, and then we just leave everything in His hands. He takes care of us, no matter what happens," Mandie tried to convince him.

"But I am not afraid," Tsa'ni rebelled.

"I'm not afraid either, really," Joe spoke up. "But I always say the verse with Mandie and the others, just to tell God I'm depending on Him."

Mandie tried to turn around and look directly at Tsa'ni at the end of the line, but the rope was too tight.

"Please, my Cherokee cousin, believe that God will protect us from harm if we ask," Mandie begged.

"No, I will not say it!" Tsa'ni snapped.

"Then we will say it without you," Dimar told him, reaching behind to take Sallie's hand. Sallie took Mandie's, and Mandie put Snowball on her shoulder to reach for Joe's hand.

The four spoke together. "What time we are afraid, we will put our trust in thee, dear God."

In a whisper Mandie added, "And dear God, please help Tsa'ni."

"Are we ready to go now?" Tsa'ni asked angrily.

"Yes, we are ready to go," Dimar answered. "Please, be careful and go very slowly. If we come to one of those places where the tracks go over a gorge, we will have to walk on the crossties."

After what seemed like hours of little progress, Dimar spotted a dangerous place ahead. "Here is one of those places," Dimar called over his shoulder. "We will have to go very slowly."

They all stopped. The tracks spanned the deep gorge in midair. And as he had said, there were only the crossties to walk on. The track was open. There was no dirt beneath it and nothing alongside it—just the width of the track supported by a bridge framework.

As they started across, Mandie made the mistake of looking down. The ground beneath dropped clear out of sight in the darkness. Her stomach turned over, and she shivered in the chilly night air. *Suppose someone's foot slipped, could the others save him—or her? It would be horrible to fall through the tracks.* She could almost feel the pain. Then she silently rebuked herself. I told God I would trust Him and here I am worrying about what might happen. Please, dear God, forgive me. I do put my trust in you.

"This is nerve-racking work," Mandie said, trying to fit her steps to the distance between the crossties without pulling or pushing the others. Everyone seemed to be holding his breath and concentrating on his feet. Snowball clung to Mandie's shoulder.

"I have done this before, lots of times," Tsa'ni bragged.

"Well, I don't think I ever want to do it again," Joe said.

"It is exhilarating up here in the air," Tsa'ni replied, throwing his hands over his head.

Mandie glanced quickly over her shoulder. "Tsa'ni!" she cried. "Please be careful!"

At that moment the Indian boy lost his footing and slipped between the crossties. Thrown off balance, he dangled in the air, trying to grasp the framework beneath the tracks.

The sudden fall jerked the others. Joe, being next to Tsa'ni, had to sit down on the crossties to keep from being pulled down with him. Mandie frantically clutched Snowball and swayed as she tried to keep from falling. Sallie and Dimar, ahead of her, did not feel the jolt quite as badly.

Dimar immediately took over. "Please sit down!" he told Sallie and Mandie. He unfastened the rope from his waist. "Hold on, Tsa'ni, hold on. I will help you."

The girls carefully sat down on the crossties next to Joe.

"Why does Tsa'ni always have to make trouble?" Joe muttered.

"Because he is a bad Cherokee," Sallie replied.

"Pray for him," Mandie urged, "so that he doesn't fall."

Dimar gingerly stepped past the other three to get to Tsa'ni.

Sallie hung her head in shame, then raised her face toward the sky. "Please, God, do not let him fall."

Mandie was looking heavenward, too. "Please take care of him, dear God," she prayed.

As Dimar knelt on the tracks and tried to reach Tsa'ni's

hand below, Joe knew he had to help, too, even though he didn't like Tsa'ni.

"Untie the rope from around y'all," Joe told the girls.

"But we might fall, too," Sallie protested.

"You won't if you sit perfectly still," Joe answered. "I need the rope for Tsa'ni."

"Of course," Mandie answered, as Sallie quickly untied the rope from her waist and passed the end to Mandie, who immediately pulled it loose from herself and passed it on back to Joe.

Dimar changed positions. "I still cannot reach you, Tsa'ni," he said.

"Wait. I'm getting the rope free," Joe told Dimar. "Then we can pull him up." He rolled up the rope and crawled back to where Dimar was stooping, trying to reach Tsa'ni.

The other end of the rope was still around Tsa'ni's waist, but it wasn't doing any good because he was hanging onto the bottom of the track with his hands, and his feet were kicking at the huge wooden post supporting the track. He kept trying to catch his toes on the post to take some of the pressure off his hands. So far he had not said a word.

Dimar helped Joe tie the rope around a crosstie and then called down to Tsa'ni.

"We have the rope secured up here and we are going to throw the end down to you. Watch for it," Dimar called to him.

Tsa'ni did not answer except to call out, "Hurry up!"

The first streaks of light began to brighten the sky. The two boys could see Tsa'ni hanging below and they threw the rope down over the side of the tracks, but it didn't go anywhere near Tsa'ni. They tried again and again but it wouldn't fall near enough for him to grab it.

"I cannot hold much longer," Tsa'ni finally said in a hoarse voice.

Mandie and Sallie sat holding hands, helplessly watching as the boys kept throwing the rope toward Tsa'ni. They silently prayed that he would be able to reach the rope.

Suddenly, Tsa'ni's hands gave way and he fell. The rope, too, broke, and the others watched in terror as he disappeared into the gorge below.

"Tsa'ni!" the boys yelled in terror.

Mandie and Sallie burst into tears, holding onto one another for comfort. Dimar and Joe looked at the dangling piece of rope. Dimar silently pulled it up and unfastened it from the crosstie.

Joe took command. "We've got to get across this thing," he said. "Then when the track is back on the ground again, we can get off and climb down there and see if we can find Tsa'ni."

"That is exactly what I was thinking," Dimar replied.

Mandie wiped her tears on her apron with one hand and held tightly to Snowball with the other. "Are Sallie and I going down after Tsa'ni, too?" Mandie asked.

Dimar looked at Joe. "Joe and I will search for him as soon as the track gets back on the ground," he answered.

"If you and Joe are going, then so am I," Mandie insisted.

"Me, too," Sallie added. "I do not wish to be left alone."

Joe looked at Dimar. "I suppose it wouldn't be safe to leave them alone, would it?"

"I guess not. They will have to go with us," Dimar agreed. "However, it will probably be very steep and rough down there."

"I'll be all right," Mandie assured them.

The sky had begun to lighten and in the growing daylight they could see that they were about halfway across the gorge. The crossties were more visible now, but the young people could also see how far below the land was.

The remaining piece of rope was not long enough to tie around them again, so they held onto it between them as they carefully walked single file down the tracks. It was a slow, scary process, but they were even more afraid of what they would find in the ravine.

Chapter 6 / Searching

As the young people neared the end of the railroad bridge, the ground gradually came up to meet them, and they breathed a little easier. The awesome trek in open space was over.

Dimar stepped from the tracks onto the ground and led the others to safety.

"Whew!" Mandie blew out her breath. "Dimar, is there any more of that kind of tracks between here and where the baggage car wrecked?"

"I do not think so," Dimar assured her with a smile. "It will get steep down the side instead." Now that it was daylight he looked at her with admiration. *She is beautiful, in spite of her grimy, tear-streaked face,* he thought.

Dimar had often looked at Mandie that way, and Joe was jealous. He spoke up quickly. "Well, suppose we try to find Tsa'ni now," he suggested.

Suddenly there was a noise on the gravel. They all turned to see Tsa'ni climbing up the hill through the thick brush.

"That will not be necessary," he said, coming toward

them. He was swinging the piece of rope that had been tied around his waist when he fell.

Everyone stared at him, unable to speak. Was that really Tsa'ni?

"I told you the rope would protect me," he laughed.

"Oh, Tsa'ni, what do you mean?" Mandie asked.

"When my hands slipped, the rope broke and I fell a great distance. But luckily, I landed in the top branches of a tree. All I had to do was get untangled and climb down," he explained, still swinging the piece of rope. "I escaped with hardly a scratch."

"And here we've been mourning for you all the time," Joe complained. "What a waste of tears!"

"You see, God did protect you," Sallie told him.

"I didn't need God. The tree broke my fall," Tsa'ni tossed back at her.

"No, Tsa'ni. God protected you. He used the tree to save you," Mandie explained.

"The *tree* saved me," the Indian boy insisted.

Joe began to walk ahead on the tracks. "There's no use in arguing with the ignorant dumbhead," he said. "We've got more important things to do, like finding Uncle Ned and the gold. Besides, I'm hungry. Let's go."

Dimar agreed. "Yes, we must hurry."

The girls followed Joe and Dimar, trying to keep up with their rapid pace. Tsa'ni lagged slightly behind the others.

"I wonder if my mother and Uncle John and Uncle Wirt got to Asheville all right," Mandie said.

"I don't imagine they stayed in Asheville if they got there," Joe told her. "They'll be out looking for us and Uncle Ned."

"I pray that my grandfather is all right," Sallie said, her voice shaking.

"Do you think he was still in the baggage car when it went off the tracks, or do you think the bandits captured him?" Dimar asked.

"I do not know what to think. It was all so sudden," Sallie answered. "But either way is bad. If my grandfather was still in the baggage car when it derailed, he may have been badly injured." She swallowed hard. "But if the bandits captured him, they may have harmed him."

"Especially since he is an Indian," Tsa'ni said bitterly.

"I can't understand why people are so prejudiced against certain other people. God made us all, and in His sight we are all equal," Mandie reasoned as they hurried along the railroad tracks.

"There are lots of people who think they are living as Christians, but they commit that sin," Dimar joined in.

"I do not claim to be a Christian, so I can say that I think the Indians are much *better* than the white people," Tsa'ni declared.

The other four were shocked.

"How can you say such a thing, Tsa'ni?" Dimar questioned.

"I am ashamed of you, Tsa'ni—as one Indian to another," Sallie told him.

"Why did you come with us in the first place?" Joe asked.

Tsa'ni did not answer.

After several moments of awkward silence, Mandie spoke. "I think the best thing we can do is to quit talking until we get to where we're going. That way, there won't be any hard feelings," she suggested.

The others agreed. Tsa'ni remained silent and trailed along behind.

At last the sun came up and the air grew warmer as the young people trudged along. Birds sang their greetings as they flew hither and yon among the trees. Now and then a butterfly flitted across their path, and once in a while a colorful wildflower peeked out of the underbrush. It was a beautiful day, but the youngsters were tired, hungry, and worried.

After a while the river and the railroad tracks came together and traveled side by side. The rushing water invited the young people to soak their tired feet, but they could not relax.

Ignoring their blisters, scratches, bruises, and sore limbs, they marched forward. At last they came around a curve where the tracks turned away from the river. And there, in the ravine below, lay the wrecked baggage car, splintered against the mountainside.

"There it is!" Mandie cried.

As exhausted as they were, they all broke into a run.

Sallie ran ahead of the others. "Grandfather!" she exclaimed, racing to the edge of the ravine.

Mandie was right behind her. When Mandie's father died, Uncle Ned had promised that he would look out for "Jim Shaw's Papoose," and now it was her turn to look out for Uncle Ned. "Please, dear God, let him be all right. Please let Uncle Ned be all right," she prayed silently.

Dimar and Joe came up behind the girls as they paused to look.

"We must go down together," Dimar told them.

"Yes," agreed Joe. "It looks kind of steep."

Tsa'ni stood alone on the tracks and watched as the others descended into the ravine. They slipped and slid until they finally reached the train car. The car lay on its side. It looked as though it had rolled over several times.

"It's so broken up I don't see how we can get inside to look for Uncle Ned," Mandie said.

"Simple," said Joe. "Dimar and I will crawl in through that hole in the side."

"But, Joe, suppose it turns over while you're in there. It's just hanging on the side of the mountain," Mandie cautioned them.

"Let it turn over," Joe answered. "It won't hurt us. We'll just tumble with it."

"May I go with you? My grandfather may be in there," Sallie begged.

"No, it is too dangerous," Dimar said. "If we find him inside we will bring him out."

The girls waited and watched while the two boys went through the hole in the train car. As the boys disappeared inside, Mandie, with Snowball on her shoulder, reached for Sallie's hand and held it tightly.

After what seemed like hours, the two boys reappeared, empty-handed. They shook their heads as they approached.

"Grandfather!" Sallie began to cry.

"Uncle Ned, where are you?" Mandie moaned.

Joe stepped forward and took Mandie's hand in his.

"I'm sorry, Mandie. He isn't there," he said to her softly. "And neither is the gold. Everything inside is completely smashed. Uncle Ned must have managed to get out somehow. Either the bandits took him or he got out on his own."

Tsa'ni, listening from where he stood, came forward to join the group. "I suggest we search immediately. If the old man is injured, he cannot be very far. That is, *if* he is still alive," he added.

At Tsa'ni's cruel remark, Sallie began to cry louder.

"Let us separate and search the surroundings," Dimar said.

"Immediately, please," Sallie begged through her tears, still holding Mandie's hand.

"Dimar, suppose you take Sallie with you, and Joe and I will go with Tsa'ni," Mandie suggested.

"Fine," Dimar replied. "If you find anything, Tsa'ni, give me a call. I will do the same. And please do not forget to watch for the bags of gold, also. They may be hard to find since they are so small."

"I would think the bandits took the gold," Joe said. "That is probably why they wrecked the train. But it wouldn't hurt to keep our eyes open."

"I will give you a whistle, Dimar, if we find anything," Tsa'ni agreed. "We will go to the left of the car and you and Sallie go right. We will meet back here when we have covered all the ground," he said.

The group separated. Mandie, with Snowball on her shoulder, followed Joe and Tsa'ni down the incline, through bramble bushes and rocks. She didn't mind the pricks and scratches. She was set on finding her dear friend, Uncle Ned.

Tsa'ni walked bent over to watch the ground for footprints or other clues. Joe and Mandie watched the bushes and trees for any sign of a trail. In the dense forest the trees grew so close together it took time to look at all of them.

"No one has come this way," Tsa'ni called over his shoulder. "But maybe we will find a trail ahead."

Mandie turned to Joe, who was walking behind her.

"Then Uncle Ned could not have come this way," she said.

"What Tsa'ni means is that no one came directly down the path we're taking," Joe explained. "Uncle Ned could have taken a path even two feet from where we are. We just have to keep walking up and down in order to cover all the area around the wrecked car. Don't give up yet."

"I won't give up. God will help us find him," Mandie said as they walked slowly forward.

"Don't say that too loudly, or we'll get a few smart remarks from Tsa'ni," Joe warned her.

"We'll have to see what we can do about Tsa'ni," Mandie said.

"I think he's hopeless," Joe replied.

"No one is hopeless, Joe. There is always hope," Mandie argued.

As they neared the river, the ground was steep and covered with slippery green moss. Mandie, trying to look all around for any sign, was not watching her step. Suddenly, her feet went out from under her and she sat down hard. Snowball, frightened by the jolt, jumped free and ran into the weeds nearby.

Joe helped her to her feet. "Are you all right?"

Mandie laughed nervously. "I'm all right," she said. "I should have been paying more attention to where I was walking. Oh, goodness, where did Snowball go?" she asked, brushing off the back of her skirt.

The two looked around quickly, but there was no sign of the white kitten. Tsa'ni did not notice their predicament and went on ahead.

Mandie searched the tall weeds. "Snowball! Kitty, kitty, kitty!" she called. "Come here, Snowball!"

The kitten meowed loudly. Joe and Mandie stood still to listen.

"He sounds either angry or hurt," Joe remarked.

"This way, Joe," Mandie said, turning to the left. "Sounds like he's over this way—toward the river."

She went on through the bushes, looking for the kitten, with Joe right behind her. The meow grew louder.

Then Snowball hopped out of the weeds in front of them. With his fur up, he meowed loudly.

"Snowball, you shouldn't run off like that," Mandie scolded. She stooped to pick him up, but he was too quick for her. He bounded into the bushes. Mandie and Joe followed. But as they came through the underbrush into the open area by the river, a terrible sight greeted them.

There on the sandy riverbank lay Uncle Ned on his back. His head was covered with blood. His bow and arrows were by his side.

Mandie, blinded with tears, rushed forward. She dropped to her knees at his side.

"Uncle Ned! Uncle Ned!" she cried, touching the still face. "Please, Uncle Ned, don't be dead! Please speak to me, Uncle Ned! Oh, dear God, please don't let him be dead!"

Joe knelt by her side and tried to find a pulse in the old man's wrist. He held his hand over Uncle Ned's mouth to see if he was breathing. He couldn't feel a thing. Jumping up, he yelled for Tsa'ni.

"Tsa'ni! Quick! Here by the river!" Joe called.

In seconds the Indian boy came rushing through the bushes.

Mandie cried as she held Uncle Ned's wrinkled hand in hers.

"Move, woman!" Tsa'ni ordered. He pushed Mandie aside to kneel by the old man. He, too, felt for a pulse and breathing with no results. "I am afraid he is very near death."

Tsa'ni stood up and gave a loud Indian call for help. Dimar and Sallie quickly joined them. When Sallie saw the condition of her grandfather, she sobbed uncontrollably.

"We must get him out of here at once!" Dimar ordered.

"Oh, dear God, how? Show us how!" Mandie said through her tears.

At that instant a faint Indian call answered Tsa'ni's. Speechless, the five young people looked at one another.

"God has sent help!" Mandie cried.

Tsa'ni gave a shrill whistle and again received an answer.

"Keep it up. Whoever it is will find us," Dimar told him.

They all waited silently, listening for the response. Each time it grew louder.

Then suddenly, Uncle Wirt burst through the bushes, followed by Uncle John, Elizabeth, Dr. Woodard, and four young Indian braves from Deep Creek and Bird-town.

Mandie rushed to Dr. Woodard, grasped his hand and pulled him down beside Uncle Ned. "Dr. Woodard, quick!" she cried.

The others gathered around as the doctor carefully examined the old Indian. Dr. Woodard looked up. "He's not dead, but he's close to it," he said gravely. "I cannot help him here, but if we don't treat him immediately, he probably will not live."

"We take him home," Uncle Wirt told them.

"It would be better if we could get him to John's house in Franklin," Dr. Woodard said. "We could care for him better there."

"Then we'll take him to my house," Uncle John declared.

Elizabeth put her arms around her daughter and tried to comfort her. But Mandie's whole body shook as she sobbed. Uncle Wirt put his arm around Sallie. It was a sad moment, always to be remembered—Uncle Ned, the dear old man, lying there helpless, and close to death.

Uncle Wirt turned to the braves and spoke rapidly in Cherokee. The young Indians immediately unrolled the blankets they carried and prepared a hammock-type bed to carry the old man over the mountain. Gently lifting him, they placed him on the blankets. Each brave took hold of a corner and lifted him from the ground. The old man did not move or utter a sound.

"Speed is the important thing," Dr. Woodard cautioned them. "We must get him to Franklin as quickly as we can."

The braves nodded in understanding.

"Braves, run!" Uncle Wirt ordered. "Quick!"

Without hesitating a second, the braves took off through the bushes, carrying the old man. Mandie and Sallie tried to follow, but Uncle John held them back.

"Wait! We have horses up at the tracks," Uncle John told them. "Since the braves left their horses, we'll have enough for all of us to ride back home."

"Braves run faster through woods than horses," Uncle Wirt said.

"Yes, they'll be there by the time we arrive," Uncle John agreed. "Thank goodness Aunt Lou and Jason Bond can help."

Mandie looked up at her mother. "Ever since we found the gold, Uncle Ned has said the gold was bad luck to the Cherokees, and now he may die because of it," she said shakily. "Oh, how could we have been so greedy that we ignored his beliefs?"

Elizabeth held her daughter tightly. "Now, don't blame yourself, dear," she said. "The gold will eventually be a good thing for the Cherokees when we get the hospital built."

"The gold is nowhere to be found," Joe informed them as they all climbed the steep side of the ravine.

The adults stopped and stared.

"So the bandits got away with it!" Uncle John said angrily.

"Cherokee catch bad men," Uncle Wirt vowed as the group hurried on up the mountainside.

Sallie looked up at Uncle Wirt. "Please catch the bad men who hurt my grandfather," she said.

Uncle Wirt took her hand in his and squeezed it gently in reply.

Riding double on some of the horses, the group galloped off toward Franklin.

Mandie fought back the tears. "Please, God, don't let him die!" she implored.

Chapter 7 / Mandie Keeps Watch

Uncle Ned, bathed and dressed in a clean nightshirt, lay very still in a bedroom across the hall from Mandie's room. Dr. Woodard tried everything he knew, but there was no improvement in the old man's condition. Finally, he sent the braves to Deep Creek to bring back Uncle Ned's squaw, Morning Star.

Everyone hovered around Uncle Ned's doorway, waiting for some word.

"I have an idea he was thrown out of the train car and landed on his head," Dr. Woodard told them. "I can't find any broken bones, though. Now that his head has been washed, you can see that there are several large cuts in the scalp."

Mandie tugged at the doctor's hand. "Dr. Woodard, will—will he—live?" she asked.

"Will he, doctor?" Sallie echoed.

"I don't know," Dr. Woodard replied. "Only the Lord knows that. I have done all I can. I'd say it's up to the Lord now."

Mandie noticed that Sallie was crying and gave her Indian friend a hug. Their tears mingled in love for the old man.

Sallie pulled Mandie across the room with her to the bed where her grandfather lay. "We will stay with him," she managed to say.

"Yes, and we will pray," Mandie said. "I know God will heal him." She held her friend's hand and they knelt by the bed.

"I think we should all pray. Come on," Elizabeth told the others. She led the way into the room and knelt behind the girls. Only Tsa'ni remained outside in the hallway. Aunt Lou, Liza, Jason Bond, and Jenny joined the others. The room was soon full of people on their knees, praying for Uncle Ned to be healed, and thanking the Lord that he had lived so far.

As the group became silent and got to their feet, Dr. Woodard spoke. "We must arrange a schedule now. He shouldn't be left alone, and I have other patients I must see now."

"I am not leaving Uncle Ned, not for one second," Mandie declared.

"Neither am I!" Sallie told them.

"But you were up all of last night, and you only ate a snack while Dr. Woodard was working with Uncle Ned," Elizabeth objected. "You two girls didn't even take a good bath when you changed clothes. You'll be Dr. Woodard's patients next if you don't take care of yourselves."

Mandie shook her head angrily. "No, no, no! I won't leave him! He would never leave me! I love him!"

"I know. I know, dear," Elizabeth said. She tried to put her arm around Mandie, but the girl pulled away. "Let's go take a nap and then you can come right back," her mother suggested.

Mandie stomped her foot. "No! I am not leaving this room!" she cried.

Elizabeth looked at her husband in despair.

"Mandie," Uncle John said firmly. "I know how much you have grown to love Uncle Ned since your father died and how Uncle Ned has been watching over you—"

Mandie wiped at her tears with her apron.

"—but we cannot permit you to throw a temper tantrum like this."

Mandie felt badly for the way she had acted and began to cry softly. Dr. Woodard understood the situation and stepped forward. "John, may I make a suggestion? Why don't you let Mandie and Sallie rest in here tonight?" He pulled one of the big, plush armchairs to the side of the bed. "That way, they can keep watch and still rest a little, too."

John thought for a moment. "Well, I suppose that would be all right. Elizabeth?" His wife nodded.

Dr. Woodard pulled a second big chair to the other side of the bed, and the girls scrambled into them. Snowball hopped up beside Mandie and curled up in a corner of the big seat. Joe took his place behind the big chair as if watching over both Uncle Ned *and* Mandie.

Elizabeth looked at John again. Mandie was her daughter, but she didn't know how to discipline her. They had never even met each other until a few months ago. She hardly knew how to be a mother. John, sensing how Elizabeth felt, and knowing Mandie didn't normally act like this, put his arm around Elizabeth and moved her toward the door.

"All right, girls," Uncle John told them. "We are going to get some sleep, but we'll be back. If you get too sleepy, Aunt Lou or Liza will take over for you."

Mandie jumped up from the chair and ran to put her arms around her mother, wiping tears from her face.

"Mother, I'm sorry." Her voice was trembling. "I love you. I do. It's just that I love Uncle Ned, too, and I have to stay here and wait. I want to be here when God heals him," she said.

Elizabeth squeezed her tightly. "I understand, dear. You and Sallie get comfortable in the chairs. We'll be back later."

As Mandie went back to her chair, John turned to Uncle Wirt, Joe, Dimar, and Tsa'ni, who was watching them from the doorway. "Come on, Uncle Wirt, boys," he said. "Aunt Lou will show you some rooms where you can rest."

Joe started to leave with the others, but quickly returned to Mandie's side.

"Do you want me to stay with you?" he asked in a low voice. "I can lie down on the rug there."

"Thank you, Joe," Mandie told him. "I appreciate your offer, but why don't you come back after you sleep?"

Joe squeezed her hand and started to go. "I'll be back soon," he promised.

Out in the hallway, Dr. Woodard gave John a slip of paper. "Here are the names of the patients I'll be seeing," he said. "If there is any change in him at all, send for me immediately. Otherwise, I'll be back as soon as I can. I'll plan on spending the night here."

"You don't really think there is any hope for him, do you?" John asked.

"Well, as I said in there, it's up to the Lord now," the doctor replied. "He does still work miracles."

"I know. We'll all be praying for him."

After everyone was settled, Aunt Lou and Liza went down to the kitchen.

"We'se gotta git my chile somethin' to eat, Liza," Aunt

Lou told the young black girl.

"Think that Injun man gonna live?" Liza asked.

Aunt Lou whirled on her heels. "Liza, don't you let me hear you talk like that agin," the old housekeeper said firmly. "That man is Mister Ned what loves my chile and watches over her. And you don't go callin' him Injun man no more. You hear that?"

"Yessum," Liza replied, looking down at the floor.

Aunt Lou pushed through the kitchen door. Jenny, the cook, was stirring something on the big iron cookstove.

"Jenny, I wants two trays loaded with some of everything you got in this kitchen," the big woman ordered.

"Two of everything, Aunt Lou?" Jenny frowned.

"Yep, two of everything you'se got cooked already, that is," Aunt Lou said. "Right now!"

"Yessum!" Jenny answered. Taking two trays from the shelf over the stove, she placed dishes on them and called for Liza. "Here, Liza, help me fill these up."

Aunt Lou supervised as Jenny and Liza opened each pot on the stove and dished up its contents.

"Now, I wants a pitcher of sweet milk," the big woman told Jenny.

"Who all's gonna eat all dis stuff?" Jenny asked, filling the milk pitcher as ordered.

"Jest my chile, and that other poor li'l girl and that smart little cat," Aunt Lou said. "He's the one what found Mister Ned. You oughta heerd what kind of troubles they done gone through."

"Yessum. Miss Amanda done told me 'bout them creatures what wrecked the train—look like ghosts," Liza told her.

"Well, shake a leg, girl. Them chillen's hungry." Aunt

Lou picked up one tray and Liza got the other one.

"I don't 'member them sayin' they'se hungry," Liza answered as she followed Aunt Lou through the doorway. "They done et one time since they got home."

"Et? They ain't et enough to keep a bird alive. I knows when my chile is hungry. She don't hafta tell me," Aunt Lou said, climbing the winding stairway to the second floor.

As they entered Uncle Ned's room with the trays, the two girls looked up.

"We'se brought my chile and her li'l friend some food," Aunt Lou said quietly. Setting the tray on a table by Mandie, she motioned for Liza to take the other tray to Sallie. Aunt Lou filled two glasses with milk and set the pitcher aside.

"Now here's enough milk for y'all and the cat," Aunt Lou said, putting the glasses on each tray.

"But, Aunt Lou, we just ate not long ago," Mandie protested.

"See what I done said? They jest et 'while ago," Liza chimed in.

Aunt Lou scowled at Liza. "Liza, you jest hesh your mouth. These chillen's gonna eat what we done brought 'em," she said.

Mandie inhaled the tempting aroma of the food. "We'll try, Aunt Lou," she said.

"Liza, go git two pillows for these chillen so's they kin curl up in dese big chairs and rest after they done et," the old woman said.

"I be right back," Liza promised, dancing quietly out of the room.

Sallie took a bite of fried okra. "The food tastes delicious, Aunt Lou," she said.

"Jenny be a good cook," Aunt Lou replied.

"Jenny is the best cook in the whole world," Mandie added.

Liza danced back into the room with two frilly pillows. As the girls sat in the big chairs eating, Liza plumped up the pillows behind them. Snowball, for once too tired to eat, stayed curled up sound asleep in the corner of Mandie's chair.

"Now, you chillen eat. We'se got work to do, but we'll be back," Aunt Lou said, waving Liza to the door.

Mandie set her tray aside and got up to give the big woman a hug. "Thank you, Aunt Lou. I love you."

The old woman bent to hug her. "I loves my chile, too, and we'se all aprayin' the good Lord spares Mister Ned's life," she said.

"Thank you, Aunt Lou," Sallie replied.

"You go finish eatin' now, Mandie," Aunt Lou ordered. "We'll be back." She closed the door quietly behind them.

When Mandie and Sallie could eat no more, they pushed their trays aside and curled up in the chairs. In spite of their determination to stay awake, before long, both of them were sound asleep. Aunt Lou, knowing this would happen, slipped back inside the room and sat down near the foot of the bed to keep watch.

Chapter 8 / Prayer Changes Things

When Morning Star arrived during the night, she fell weeping upon her husband's bed. Only Mandie and Sallie could calm her.

Mandie knelt with the old squaw and Sallie by the bed. "Morning Star, Uncle Ned is not going to die," she said. "God is going to heal him."

Morning Star couldn't understand everything Mandie was saying, so Sallie translated it into Cherokee.

"God is testing our faith, Morning Star. We must put our faith in God to heal Uncle Ned," Mandie continued. "I believe He will answer our prayers."

As Morning Star calmed down, she took her husband's hand and began to pray in the Cherokee language. Refusing to leave the room to eat or sleep, she stayed with Mandie and Sallie as they watched and waited.

Every day Dr. Woodard came to examine Uncle Ned. But on the third day he sadly shook his head. He turned to John Shaw who was standing nearby.

"I'm afraid we're going to lose him," the doctor said.

Hearing his words, Mandie ran to the bedside and began to cry. She grabbed the old man's hands in hers and shook him.

"Uncle Ned! Uncle Ned! Come back to me. Please don't die!" she cried hysterically, tears streaming down her cheeks.

Sallie knelt beside her grandmother to explain in Cherokee what the doctor had just said.

Morning Star looked up at Dr. Woodard. "God heal. No die," she said firmly.

Uncle John tried to settle Mandie down. But as he reached to pull her hands away from the old man's, Mandie cried out in joy.

"Uncle Ned! Uncle Ned, I knew you wouldn't leave me," she exclaimed.

They all hovered closely around the bed, astonished to see his eyes open. Uncle Ned looked directly at Mandie, then curled his fingers around her hand.

Dr. Woodard reached for the old Indian's wrist, waited silently for a moment, then smiled. "His pulse is normal," he announced. "God still works miracles."

"Grandfather, I love you," Sallie whispered.

Morning Star gently rubbed his forehead. "God heal," she muttered.

Uncle Ned managed a slight smile for his wife and granddaughter. "Eat," he said softly.

Everyone laughed and began to praise God. Aunt Lou hurried Jenny into making some hot broth for the old man. Before long Morning Star was holding his head and feeding him with a spoon.

Uncle Ned continued to improve a little bit each day. As soon as he was able, he told them what had happened to him. Propped up on his pillows, and with everyone gathered around him in great anticipation, he began his story.

"Ghosts ride horses," he said. "Train stop. They unhook train. Baggage car roll backward. Go off track. I jump out. Hurt head. Get water. No more remember."

There were lots of questions, and the young people told him what they had been through. But no one knew what happened to the gold.

Several days later, when Uncle Ned was well enough to sit up in a chair, Mandie waited until everyone else was out of the room, and then came to sit on the rug at his feet. Leaning her head against his knee, she said, "Uncle Ned, I need to talk to you. Are you well enough to talk?"

He nodded and smiled. "Well enough to get up and go," he said.

"I've been thinking a lot since you got hurt," the girl began. "You know, the gold is all gone. I guess the bandits stole it. But you know what I think?" She looked up at him very seriously. "I think God took it all away from us because we forgot to tithe. We forgot to give Him ten percent of it."

Uncle Ned was startled with her thinking. "No, no, no, Papoose!" he said anxiously. "Big Book say Big God throw blessings out window to people if people tithe."

"But we didn't tithe," Mandie said.

"Then we no get blessings," the old man replied. "But Big God not punish. Papoose find gold, but bad men take it away—not Big God."

"Do you really think so? I've been so worried about it," she said.

"So. Bad men take gold—not Big God," the old Indian repeated. "Cherokee find bad men, get gold back for Papoose."

"Oh, I hope we can get it back. I want so much to build that hospital for the Cherokees," Mandie told him.

"And if we get it back, we will most certainly give ten percent of it to the Lord."

The old man smiled and patted her blonde head. "Then we must watch so we catch. Blessings fall down on us from window up there." Uncle Ned pointed upward.

Mandie felt better after her conversation with her dear friend. She knew Uncle Ned was right. And now that he was so much better she had time for her friends.

During those first trying days, Joe had more or less been her shadow, and of course, Sallie was always with Mandie and Uncle Ned. But it seemed that Dimar and Tsa'ni had done nothing but sit around and eat. Leaving Morning Star with Uncle Ned, Mandie decided to round up her friends. She found them all together in the parlor.

As Mandie entered the room, Polly Cornwallis, her friend from next door, rushed up and put her arms around her.

"Mandie, I was so sorry to hear about everything," she said, shaking her black curls out of her eyes. "Mother and I have been in Nashville. We just got back this afternoon."

"I'm glad you came, Polly," Mandie told her. "Have you met all my friends?"

Whirling about to smile at Joe, Polly replied, "Yes, Joe just finished introducing all of us."

"Well, then, since Uncle Ned is so much better, and Morning Star is staying with him for a while," Mandie explained, "I thought you might all like to see the secret tunnel Joe and I have told you about."

The others were on their feet immediately.

"Yes, yes," Dimar answered.

"Oh, please," Sallie chimed in.

"It would be interesting," Tsa'ni said.

Joe came to Mandie's side. "I'll be the guide for you,"

he laughed as he led the way into the hall. "Hadn't we better get the key from your Uncle John?"

Sticking her hand in her apron pocket, Mandie withdrew a large key and held it up. "I already have."

Snowball bounced along under their feet as Joe led the way up the stairs to the third floor and into Uncle John's library. The young Indians were fascinated with the beautiful house. They had never seen such a large mansion before.

Joe walked over to the heavy draperies in the corner of the room and pulled them aside, revealing a door. Mandie inserted the key and swung it open. Behind the door was a paneled wall. Pushing a latch, she waited for the panel to swing aside and then showed them steps going down.

Dimar was impressed. "That is very clever," he said.

"I think so, too," Mandie said with pride. "Uncle John said my great-grandfather built this house when the Cherokees were being moved out of North Carolina. He didn't like the way they were being treated, so he had this tunnel built just for them. He hid as many Cherokees as he could in this tunnel until things became peaceful. It was about 1842 when the Indians moved out and set up their own living quarters," Mandie explained. She turned to Tsa'ni. "That's how my grandfather and my grandmother met," she said. "He was twenty-eight, and she was a beautiful eighteen-year-old Indian girl. So you see, my family not only married Indians, they helped them survive when no one else would."

Tsa'ni only tightened his lips and said nothing.

Sallie sighed. "What a beautiful romance!"

"Yes," Mandie agreed. "My grandmother was Uncle Wirt's sister, you know. So he is really my great-uncle."

"Let's go," Tsa'ni complained.

Joe led them through the door to the steps. "It's kind of dark in places," he cautioned, "so be sure to watch your step."

Snowball meowed at Joe's feet. Joe picked up the cat and handed him to Mandie.

As they made their way through, Sallie and Dimar were thrilled, knowing the tunnel had once protected their people. When they finally emerged in the woods, almost out of sight of the house, they were really excited.

"What an adventure!" Dimar exclaimed, looking back to the exit door concealed by bushes.

Sallie turned to Mandie. "You know that my grandfather and my grandmother lived here at one time, don't you?"

Mandie set Snowball down and the kitten rubbed around her ankles. "Yes, Uncle John told me. Morning Star and Uncle Ned came to live with them after my grandfather died. He said my father was only five years old then," Mandie replied.

"My grandfather has never mentioned this tunnel to me," Sallie said. "He lived here, so he must have known about it."

"Your grandfather is the world's greatest keeper of secrets!" Mandie laughed.

"The old people do not like to talk about the Cherokee removal, or anything that reminds them of it," Dimar volunteered.

Tsa'ni changed the subject. "When are they going to look for the gold?" he asked.

Everyone stared at him.

"Who is going to look for the gold?" Joe asked.

"My grandfather and Mandie's uncle are planning to," Tsa'ni answered.

Mandie stood up straighter. "The Cherokees put me in charge of the gold, so I will go with them to hunt for it," she told them.

"So will I," Joe put in.

"And I," Sallie said.

Dimar was again admiring Mandie's pretty blue eyes. "I also would like to go with you," he said.

"Could I go, too?" Polly asked. "I'd just love to look for those creatures that stole it."

"Oh, Polly!" Mandie replied. "It won't be fun. They were awfully dangerous looking."

"Joe already told me about them," Polly said. "Do you think I could go with you?"

"I suppose. You'd have to ask your mother and also my Uncle John," Mandie said.

"Then let's go find out," Polly said, turning to go up the hill to the house.

The young people found Uncle John with Uncle Wirt and Elizabeth in the parlor. Not waiting for any greeting or explanation, Polly walked straight to Uncle John and asked, "Could I please go with y'all to search for the gold?"

Uncle John looked at her and then at the other youngsters.

"Do what?" he asked.

"You are making plans to hunt the gold, and everyone else is going, so I'd like to go, too," Polly explained.

"Now wait a minute," Uncle John said, addressing the anxious young people. "This business about the gold must be kept absolutely secret. No one is to know about it outside of our immediate group here. If it got to be public knowledge, we'd have half the country out here looking for it. We'd never find it. Do you all understand?"

They nodded in agreement.

Mandie sat down on a low stool near her uncle. "But, are we going to look for it?" Mandie asked.

"Uncle Wirt and I will," John answered.

"But, Uncle John, I am responsible for the gold. My Cherokee kinpeople put me in charge of it, so I must go, too," Mandie pleaded.

"It's too dangerous," Uncle John told her.

"I'm not afraid," Mandie protested. "I have to find it so I can give ten percent of it to the Lord, and we can receive His blessings."

"You can give the ten percent after Uncle Wirt and I find it," he reasoned.

Just then Snowball came into the room and jumped into Mandie's lap. That gave Mandie an idea. "I have to go so Snowball can go," she said. "Remember, he was the one who found Uncle Ned. Maybe he can help us find the bandits."

No one dared to laugh.

"Amanda, darling," Elizabeth said gently, "I want you to stay here with me to help take care of Uncle Ned. Please."

"But, Mother, Uncle Ned said we must find the gold so we can tithe," Mandie told her. "And he can't go, so I have to."

Uncle John finally relented. "All right, you youngsters can go with us to the wrecked train car, but I don't make any promises after that," he told them. Turning to Joe, he added, "If we get that far we'll stop at your father's house, Joe. He must be home by now."

"John, are you going to permit this?" Elizabeth asked in disbelief. "You know I don't want Amanda to go."

"I never could resist blue eyes!" he laughed. "Especially when they're so much like yours."

The young people dashed out of the room and ran over to Polly's house to ask her mother's permission. After a lot of talking, they finally convinced her that it was not dangerous, and that they were only going to the wrecked train car. Polly went home with Mandie to spend the night so they could start out early the next morning.

Mandie was excited about the trip to the wrecked baggage car, but would they ever really find the gold again?

Chapter 9 / Off to Find the Gold

Before sunrise the young people quietly slipped out of bed and gathered in the kitchen. Jenny was busy preparing breakfast and food for the journey. Since Elizabeth was not going, Uncle John had told Liza she could go along to look after the three girls. Liza was so excited she danced around in circles among them while their conversation grew louder and louder.

Aunt Lou heard the commotion and came into the kitchen. "You best be quietenin' down or Mr. John'll be in here to see what's goin' on! Liza, 'member youse jest goin' to take care of my chile and these heah other li'l girls."

"Yessum," Liza calmed down. "I behave. I see to Miss Amanda and Miss Sallie and Miss Polly. I see they behave, too."

Mandie laughed. She knew the trip would be more fun with Liza along. "And I'll see that Liza behaves," she said mischievously.

"Lawsy, Missy," Liza said. "I ain't got nobody sweet on me to go smoochin' with."

Everyone broke into laughter.

"Git outa heah," Aunt Lou said, shooing the young people out through the door. "Git yo' breakfast in the dinin' room. Liza be bringin' it in a minute."

Mandie was the last one out of the kitchen. "Can Liza eat with us, Aunt Lou?" she asked.

"Hesh yo' mouth, chile. Liza don't belong in the dinin' room," the big woman told her.

"But, Aunt Lou, Liza's going to eat with us on the trip. She has to, or eat somewhere by herself," Mandie insisted.

"Well, that won't be under the roof of Mr. John's house," Aunt Lou told her. "While she under Mr. John's roof, she gonna act like the servant girl she be. Now, git on in there wid yo' friends."

"I just don't understand it, Aunt Lou," Mandie argued. "Why can't she eat with us? When I lived at my father's house in Swain County everyone ate at the same table."

"You'll understand some day, my chile. Now git!" the old woman said.

Mandie sat down at the big dining room table with her friends. Before long her mother and Uncle John and Uncle Wirt joined them.

"Uncle John, why can't Liza eat breakfast with us?" Mandie asked, as soon as her uncle was seated. "After all, she'll have to eat with us on the trip."

Liza came through the doorway with huge platters of scrambled eggs, bacon, ham, and grits. "Oh, you want Liza to eat with us?" Uncle John asked. Looking up at the young servant girl, he said, "Liza, you get a plate and sit down over there next to Mandie. We're all in this thing together beginning today."

Liza almost dropped the platters as she set them down. "What, Mister John?" she gasped.

"Mandie wants you to eat with us since you're going on the journey too. So get yourself a plate and sit down," Uncle John told her.

"Yes, Liza, sit right here next to me." Mandie used her foot to push out the chair next to her.

"Missy, I can't do that. Aunt Lou, she git all over me," Liza protested.

"But Uncle John is the boss here. You heard what he said. Get your plate," Mandie insisted.

Liza gave up. "Yes, Missy, I git me a plate and be right back," the black girl said, returning to the kitchen.

Elizabeth looked at John.

"I told you I just can't resist those blue eyes, especially when they look so much like yours," John told her.

"First thing you know, you'll have all the servants in an uproar," Elizabeth protested. "The other servants won't like the idea at all."

"Leave it to me. I'll take care of it if and when that time comes," John told her. "After all, I'm half Indian. I'm not expected to act in the usual 'white people' fashion," he laughed.

"Oh, John, you can be funny!" Elizabeth smiled.

Polly was sitting next to Mandie and gave her a nudge. "Mandie, you have some great parents!" she said.

"One parent," corrected Mandie. "Uncle John is still my uncle, even though he is married to my mother."

"They are very much in love," Dimar said, helping himself to more eggs and bacon.

She missed her father so much, it was hard to sort out her feelings about all that happened.

Uncle John was the "richest man this side of Richmond," according to Liza. Why hadn't he shared his wealth with her father who was desperately poor? She would always wonder about that.

Liza came back through the door with a plate in one hand and a platter of hot biscuits in the other. After putting the biscuits in the middle of the long table, she sat down next to Mandie.

"Here," Mandie said. She reached for the platter of eggs and passed it to Liza.

Joe passed the bacon and ham.

Dimar watched in amusement from the other end of the table. "Eat," he said.

"That's one word that's good in any language—eat," Joe laughed.

Liza nervously helped herself to the food, and then sat there pushing the food around with her fork. She cast a sheltered glance now and then at the others at the table.

"Liza, eat," Uncle John's voice boomed from the other end of the table. "We've got to get going."

"Yes, sir. Yes, sir, Mister John," Liza answered and quickly shoved her mouth full of food.

Sallie looked across the table at Liza and felt sorry for her. *Poor Liza!* she thought. *She's so nervous sitting at the big table that she can't eat.* She almost choked on the food and hurried to wash it down with coffee that was too hot.

"Please do not worry. We are all on your side," Sallie told her. "I felt the same way the first time I sat at this great table in this fancy house. You see, I live in a log cabin with my grandfather and grandmother."

"I ain't never lived in a log cabin, Miss Sallie," Liza replied. "I wouldn't know how to act in a log cabin."

All the young people laughed.

"I also live in a log cabin," Dimar told her.

"And so do I," Tsa'ni added.

Turning to Mandie, Liza asked, "Where all these log cabins at?"

"Liza, haven't you ever seen a log cabin?" Mandie asked. "You know I lived in a log cabin with my father, too. That's how people live out in the country away from town. Log cabins are scattered all over the woods and fields."

"I ain't never lived in de country either. I be born right heah in this house," Liza told them.

"You were?" Mandie said. "Where are your mother and father?"

"They be done dead with de new-moanie, long time ago, when I was a li'l tyke. Aunt Lou, she tuck care of me after that," Liza told them.

"My father died from the same thing," Mandie said.

Uncle John's voice boomed out again. "Eat up, everyone! Whoever is going with me, be ready in fifteen minutes."

He got up and left the table, with Elizabeth and Uncle Wirt following.

"You heard him. Eat," Joe said. "Let's hurry and get done!"

Liza tried her best to swallow the food. She *was* hungry, but to have to sit here with "Miss Amanda" and her friends was too much for her. She pushed her plate away and stood up.

"I'se done," she said. "Let's git our things and go."

Mandie looked at the girl's plate. "But, Liza, you hardly ate anything at all," Mandie objected.

Liza turned to her and spoke softly. "To be honest 'bout it, Miss Amanda, I jest didn't wanta eat in here with all these people. It'd be like you eatin' with Mr. McKinley in the White House."

"You really mean that, don't you, Liza?" Mandie replied. "I'm sorry if I spoiled your breakfast. I won't do it again."

"That's all right, Missy. Next time I eat in the kitchen where I belongs," Liza replied.

When they got outside, Uncle John had horses and ponies tethered at the front gate, loaded with blankets, rope, lanterns, and food. The adults stood waiting on the front porch. Elizabeth caught Mandie by the arm.

"Amanda, you haven't put on your riding outfit," she reprimanded.

"But, Mother. Sallie doesn't have one on, and neither do Polly and Liza," Mandie protested.

"I told my mother we were riding in a wagon," Polly explained. "I didn't know we were going to ride ponies. But it's all right. She won't mind."

Elizabeth frowned at her husband. "John, we need to teach Amanda some proper manners for young ladies," she said.

John laughed. "Why don't we let it go this time? It'll be quicker and safer in that rough mountain terrain if they all ride astride. Seems like I remember *you* saying the same thing not too long ago." He kissed Elizabeth on the cheek.

Elizabeth gave in. "It seems like I always come out on the losing end," she said with a little laugh.

Mandie took her mother by the hand. "Please tell Uncle Ned we'll be back soon," she said. "I didn't want to wake him this early in the morning to tell him good-bye."

"Of course, dear," Elizabeth answered. She gave her daughter a squeeze. "Be a good girl."

"Everybody ready?" Uncle John asked. "Run and find yourselves a pony."

Mandie picked up Snowball and rushed out to the road with the others to claim her pony. Mandie knew she had to help Liza feel comfortable with them. "Liza! Here! Get this pony next to mine!" she called.

Liza gratefully did as Mandie said.

Waving good-bye to Elizabeth, Aunt Lou, and Jenny, the group took off down the road.

A long time later, they approached the place in the railroad tracks where they knew the wrecked baggage car would be. As they drew rein and looked down the ravine, they spotted the wrecked baggage car still hanging onto the side of the mountain.

"We walk from here," Uncle Wirt told them.

Dismounting, they followed him carefully down the slope.

"Watch for trail marking," he said.

"Here is where we went down to the wrecked car," Dimar said, pointing to the spot. "Then we split up, and Sallie and I went over this way," he continued. "Tsa'ni took Mandie and Joe over that way and we all met at the river where we found Uncle Ned."

"When we came in answer to your call, we must have taken almost the same path then, Dimar," Uncle John replied. "That's a lot of shoes making prints in the dirt."

Suddenly, Uncle Wirt stooped to examine the ground. "Boot make this mark," he said, pointing to a firm print in the dirt. "We no wear boot!"

Uncle John bent to look at it. "You're right. That's the print of a hard heel and pointed toe, like riding boots."

"Him go this way." Uncle Wirt walked closer to the baggage car. "Then on. All way to train car."

"Great!" Joe said.

Mandie started looking around, holding Snowball

tightly in her arms. "Now if we can find the same prints going *away* from the car . . ."

The group fanned out and soon Dimar called, "Here is the same print going toward the river."

Uncle Wirt found more. "Horses been here. Go up riverbank," he said.

"Yes," Mandie told him. "There were three of them. They came from all different directions."

"Do you want to look inside the baggage car in case we missed something?" Joe asked.

"It looks like it might roll away," Uncle John speculated.

"We went inside, and it did not move," Dimar told him. "It is leaning against big bushes on the other side."

Uncle Wirt headed for the broken place in the side of the car where the young people had entered before. He tried to shake the car, but it wouldn't move. He climbed up and went inside. Uncle John, Dimar and Joe followed right behind him, but Tsa'ni stayed outside with the girls.

Liza surveyed the wreck. "Lawsy mercy, Missy. Thank the Lawd youse didn't go down the mountain wid dat car," she said.

"Yes, we have plenty to be thankful for," Mandie replied.

"Did you see it fall down the mountain like that?" Polly asked.

"No, but we heard the crash. This is the car my grandfather was in," Sallie told her.

"Oh, dat pore man!" Liza moaned. "So now we's gonna find the bad men what wrecked the train and hurt your grandfather?"

"We will *try* to find them," the Indian girl said.

"Won't you be afraid if we do?" Polly asked.

"No, I will not be afraid. We have all these big, strong men with us now," Sallie replied.

"I'd just like to catch up with them, for all the trouble they've caused," Mandie said.

Tsa'ni clenched his fists. "But they were white men and we are Indians," he said to Sallie. "We cannot do anything to them."

"That's what you think," Mandie told him. "You just wait and see what happens if we find them. Uncle John will see to that."

"Well, since he is living as a white man and not like an Indian, he can prosecute them, I suppose," the Indian boy replied.

"You know he is half Cherokee, but he can live as he chooses. So can you and all the other Cherokees," Mandie informed him.

"You certainly do not know much about it, do you?" the boy told her. "Someday you will find out what it means to be Indian by white people's standards."

When the men and the other boys came out of the wrecked car, the girls stared in amazement. Joe ran toward them wearing a tiger face mask like the bandits had worn.

"Joe, stop that!" Mandie gasped. "Was that mask in there?"

He nodded.

"It does not look so scary in the daylight," Sallie told them.

"Well, I'd sure hate to meet that thing in the dark," Polly declared.

"I'd be done passed out if that thing come toward me in de dark," Liza told them, moving away from Joe.

Joe took another step toward her and raised his arms.

"Liza, there were three of them. And it was dark. And they wore long, flowing cloaks and big hats," he teased.

Liza backed off. "Git 'way from heah!" she squealed.

Dimar came up and took the mask from Joe. "We did not find this mask when we went inside last time, because everything was broken and thrown around. But the railroad must have come since then and taken all the broken baggage out. All that is left is trash," he told the girls.

Uncle John and Uncle Wirt joined them in their discussion.

"That mask proves the bandits were in the baggage car," Uncle John reasoned.

Uncle Wirt nodded. "We trace hoof prints," he said.

Uncle John started for the horses. "We're going to see if we can follow their trail," he told the young people. "Coming?"

No one had to be asked twice. Back at the riverbank, they began the tedious job of tracking the bandits' horses.

The closer they got to the gold, the more danger awaited them.

Chapter 10 / A Visit to Charley Gap

Uncle Wirt managed to pick up enough tracks in the dirt to follow the bandits' trail. Slowly and carefully, he led the way over the mountain.

The trail ride was fun for the young people. And, as Mandie had expected, Liza turned out to be the life of the search party.

"I ain't never been outside Franklin," Liza told them. "I thought the whole world was a city with lots of houses and people, but we ain't seen a soul 'cept us since we left the road. I wouldn't wanta live out heah." Her eyes opened wide. "I'd be askeered them bears and panthers and things would come and git me."

"When we see one, we'll let you know, Liza," Joe teased.

The black girl looked startled. "You mean we might come close to some of them things?"

"We might see anything in a forest like this," Dimar answered. "But I brought my bow and arrows. So did Tsa'ni and his grandfather. You are well protected. We will not let anything harm you."

Joe patted the rifle slung over his pony. "And Mr. Shaw and I are carrying rifles," he assured her.

Tsa'ni sat up taller in his saddle. "I also have a rifle, as well as my bow and arrows," he said.

"So you double smart," Liza told him. She turned to Mandie. "Missy, don't you think we oughta brought us a gun, too?"

Mandie laughed. "No, Liza, we might shoot somebody."

"But we could shoot the bandits," Liza said.

"No, no," Sallie protested. "We only want to capture them and turn them over to the law."

Polly gradually maneuvered her pony through the group until she was riding ahead next to Joe.

Seeing this, Liza leaned over to Mandie and whispered, "You better watch Miss Sweet Thing. She be after your Mister Joe."

Mandie laughed and then strained her neck to watch the two ahead. They seemed to be joking and talking as they rode along together. A pang of jealousy cut through her, but she could not let Liza know it.

"Oh, Liza, he's not my Mister Joe," Mandie told her. "He can talk to anybody he wants to."

"It ain't him, Missy, that I'm a'talkin' 'bout. It's that Miss Sweet Thing. She shore is tryin' to latch onto him," Liza warned.

"Polly is my friend, and she's also Joe's friend," Mandie replied.

"You jest watch what I'm a'sayin'," Liza insisted. "She layin' it on so thick the bees git drownded in it."

Mandie smiled but did not answer. Adjusting Snowball to a higher position on her shoulder, she petted the kitten thoughtfully. She knew Polly was interested in Joe, but she wasn't worried. She had known Joe all her life. Of course, Mandie was jealous when Polly flirted with Joe, but she tried not to let it bother her. She was sure Polly would eventually find someone else to "latch onto," as Liza called it.

Up ahead, the men stopped, and the young people hurried to catch up. John and Uncle Wirt dismounted and stood in a grassy spot, by a sparkling spring where the horses could drink.

"Eat now!" Uncle Wirt announced. "Must water ponies."

Taking their food bags from their ponies, the young people tethered the animals where they could graze near the water. Sitting on the rocks by the spring, they enjoyed the ham and biscuits, boiled eggs, and apples that Jenny had packed for them.

Uncle John came to sit by Mandie. "Uncle Wirt has tracked them this far, but we thought we'd better stop to rest and eat." He paused, then looked directly at her. "Do you know where we are?" he asked.

Mandie glanced at him and then around the forest, trying to find a familiar landmark.

"Uncle John!" she cried, grabbing his big hand. A tear trickled down her cheek.

Her uncle took out a big handkerchief. "Don't cry, dear," he said, wiping her tears. "You do know where we are, don't you?"

"Yes, yes, Uncle John." Mandie's voice trembled. "My father's grave is right over the hill up there and—and—his—house is not far away."

"I wanted you to know before we got there. I didn't want it to be a sudden shock," Uncle John said. "We'll stop when we get there, and I'll help you find some flowers to put on his grave."

Mandie buried her face on his chest as he hugged her to him.

Joe overheard the conversation, but had already realized where they were. He passed the word to the others, and they all became silent.

Uncle John got up and spoke to Joe. "We're planning to spend the night at your father's house tonight."

"Great!" Joe exclaimed.

When the others began to talk among themselves, Joe slipped away from the crowd and went to Mandie, who was sitting alone now, except for Snowball. He took her hand in his and squeezed it.

"Mind if I ride beside you?" he asked. "I know you've been trying to stay with Liza to make her feel comfortable. But if you don't mind, I'd like to be with you when we ride up over that hill," he said gently.

Mandie leaned forward and took his other hand in hers. "Of course, Joe. I want you to," she said with a smile.

After they mounted again, Joe and Mandie rode directly behind Uncle John. At the top of the hill, when the cemetery came into sight, the others stopped and waited. They knew Mandie wanted to be alone.

Mandie slid down from her pony, handed Snowball to Uncle Wirt, and took Joe and Uncle John by the hand. Together they walked among the graves until they came to the one with a homemade marker reading: "James Alexander Shaw; Born April 3, 1863; Died April 13, 1900." The mound had flattened some, and it was covered with grass. A handful of wilted flowers stuck out of a clay pot next to the marker.

Mandie let go of their hands and fell on her knees by her father's grave. Tears blurred her vision.

"Daddy, I still love you. I haven't forgotten you. I never will!" she cried softly.

Uncle John knelt by her side and put his arm around her. "Just remember that he's in heaven, darling. And one day you can see him there," he assured her.

"I know, I know! But I miss him! I loved him so much!" she said between sobs.

"I loved him, too, dear. He was the only brother I had." Uncle John stood up to pull a handkerchief from his pocket and wiped his eyes.

Joe squatted next to Mandie. "I'm sorry those flowers are dead," he apologized. "I know I promised you I would keep flowers on the grave, but I haven't been home for a long time. Want to look for some now?"

Mandie nodded, wiping her tears on her apron as Joe helped her up. "Yes, let's find some pretty flowers," she said, taking their hands.

Strolling around the edge of the cemetery, they picked several bunches of Indian Paintbrush and carried them back to replenish the clay pot.

Uncle John stared at the grave with its crude marker. "Mandie, we're going to have a real tombstone put on your father's grave, a granite one," he said.

Mandie smiled up at her uncle with tears glistening in her eyes. "One with a flower pot attached, so we can keep lots of flowers here?"

"Anything you want, darling. As soon as we can get time we'll go to Asheville and look at some," he promised. "Now I think we'd better go back and join the others. We have to pass awfully close to your father's house in order to get to Dr. Woodard's."

"We do?" She looked surprised and then added, "I

suppose you do have to go down that road to get to Dr. Woodard's house."

"Yes," Uncle John replied. "But I know how much trouble your stepmother has caused. We're going to try to stay out of sight."

Joe helped Mandie mount her pony. "I haven't forgotten, Mandie," he said. "I'll get your father's house back for you when we grow up. Remember, I promised I would?"

"Oh, I hope you can, Joe," the girl answered.

Joe stayed close to Mandie from then on.

In her mind, Mandie relived the day their old horse, Molly, had pulled the wagon bearing her father's coffin up the hill to the cemetery. She also painfully remembered the empty ride back down. Silently, she thanked God for sending Uncle Ned to her. He had promised her father to watch over her and he kept his promise. He always turned up just when she needed him. Mandie wished he could have come with them, but Uncle John had insisted he was not well enough for the rough journey.

"Ps-s-st!" Joe leaned over and pointed. Her father's house was barely visible through the trees. They stopped their ponies and those behind them waited. The men looked back and slowed down.

"Just think," Mandie sighed, "all my life, I grew up believing that woman living there was my mother. Then my father died, and Uncle John showed me the truth. But I will always wonder why my father didn't tell me," she said sadly.

Joe's pony snickered and bumped into Mandie's pony, giving it a jolt. Snowball didn't like being jostled around on Mandie's shoulder, and he jumped down.

"Snowball! Come back here!" Mandie called. She slid

down from the pony and tried to catch him. Joe quickly dismounted to help. But the kitten wanted to play games. Snowball ran and stopped until he thought they were going to try to pick him up. Then he ran again, too quick for them to catch him.

Everyone watched silently. Uncle Wirt had warned them that they must not be seen or heard by anyone at the log cabin in the hollow below.

"Snowball, come here!" Mandie tried to coax him. "Here, kitty, kitty, kitty!"

But Snowball had a mind of his own. He turned to look at her, meowed loudly, and then bounded through the trees toward the house below. Mandie and Joe started after him, but stopped in the shelter of the bushes at the edge of the clearing. The kitten went on.

As they watched from the bushes, they could see and hear someone talking. Moving to get a better view, Mandie's heart beat wildly. Her stepsister, Irene, and her boyfriend, Nimrod, sat on a stump by the side of the house.

"Nimrod, quit holdin' onto me so tight. It hurts," Irene protested.

"I jest wanna be near you," Nimrod answered.

Mandie looked around in despair. How would she ever get her kitten back? Snowball was roaming the yard below. Glancing up the hill, she noticed Uncle John motioning for her to come.

"We'll get Polly to go down and get Snowball," he said. "They've never seen her, so they won't know who she is."

"Maybe she can slip down there and get him before they see her," Mandie suggested.

"She can try, and we'll watch from here," Uncle John said.

Polly gladly consented, and cautiously made her way down the hill into the yard. The two on the stump had not seen the kitten. Snowball was nosing around a flower bed nearby. Polly eased up to him, but when she reached to pick him up, he let out a yowl. She quickly squeezed him in her arms so he couldn't get down. Irene and Nimrod immediately turned around and saw Polly with the kitten.

Irene jumped up. "Who are you? What you doin' here?"

"I just lost my cat," Polly mumbled as Nimrod towered over her. She turned to go, but Irene grabbed her by her black braid.

"Not so fast. This jest don't sound right to me," Irene told her.

The group on the hill watched breathlessly. Mandie was about to go down and rescue Polly when a loud yell startled her.

"Irene! Irene, where you at?" Irene's mother called from the back door. "Irene!"

Irene immediately let go of Polly. "Quick, Nimrod! Behind the barn!" she whispered. "Don't let Mama see you! I'll be back out soon as I kin git away from Mama. Wait fer me." Her mother continued yelling as Irene ran to the house.

Quick as lightning, Polly ran up the hill and disappeared into the trees. She didn't stop running until she reached Mandie and handed her the kitten.

Polly laughed. "Whew! That was a close call!" she said, trying to catch her breath.

Mandie put her arm around her friend. "Thank you, Polly. You don't know how much I appreciate that," she told her.

"That woman is your stepmother?" Polly asked.

"Yes, and that's her daughter, Irene," Mandie replied. "I lived in that house with them most of my life."

The weary group continued on. By the time they passed through Charley Gap and stopped in back of Dr. Woodard's house, the sun had disappeared beyond the mountains. When the doctor and Mrs. Woodard heard the commotion outside, they came into the yard to greet them.

"Light and come in!" Dr. Woodard called.

"Oh, Joe!" Mrs. Woodard cried, "it's so good to have you home."

Joe gave his mother a hug as his dog, Samantha, and her four puppies excitedly ran rings around him. Mandie had to back away from them and hold her kitten. Snowball didn't like the dogs at all, so Mandie hurried inside.

Dr. Woodard's house was made of logs like the others in the area, but it had two stories. Upstairs, there were four bedrooms, crammed full of huge beds with headboards that almost reached the ceiling. Mr. and Mrs. Miller, who lived in a cabin down the hill on the Woodards' property, helped out around the house.

Before long, Mrs. Woodard and Mrs. Miller had a delicious supper cooked and on the table. The young people ate as though they hadn't had a bite to eat for a month. Liza was still uncomfortable eating with the others, and offered to clean up the kitchen.

But Mrs. Woodard shooed all of them out.

"No, we don't need any help," she told them. "You young people just go out on the porch, or make yourselves comfortable somewhere, and rest. I know what you've been through today."

Mandie wandered outside to sit on the porch steps in the bright moonlight. Liza sat down beside her.

"Lawsy, Missy, if Aunt Lou knowed whut I be doin', sittin' at other people's tables and eatin' and then not even cleanin' up the dishes, she'd wring my neck. I could've at least put the vittles up instead of lollygaggin' around here doin' nothin'," Liza told her.

Sallie and Dimar came out and sat in the porch swing while Tsa'ni walked into the yard to play with the dogs.

"You see, Liza, I told you everybody sits at the same table to eat where I come from," Mandie said happily.

"Well, that ain't my style, I guess," Liza replied. "I think dat woman oughta let me do sumpin'."

Just then, Joe came out the door, overhearing what Liza said. "Liza," he said, "my mother considers you a guest in our house same as all these other people, and you sure don't go letting guests wash dishes."

Polly stood at the doorway. "Hey, Joe, how about showing me your horse that you told me about?"

"All right," he said. "Mandie? Liza? Y'all want to go, too?"

Before Mandie could answer, Uncle John called to her from inside. "Mandie, will you come inside for a minute?"

"Of course, Uncle John," Mandie answered. "I'll catch up with you later, Joe."

Mandie glanced at Liza, who made a face. Mandie sighed and then went inside. Joe and Polly were off to the barn. She felt that pang of jealousy again, and wished Liza would go with them.

Inside, Mandie looked around the finely-furnished living room.

Mrs. Woodard motioned toward the settee between her and Uncle John. "Sit down, dear. I won't keep you but a minute," she said. "I just wanted to give you some information for your mother."

"Yes, ma'am," Mandie replied as she sat down by the gentle, attractive woman who looked just a little older than her mother.

Mrs. Woodard handed her some papers. "This is information about the school your mother asked me to look into when I went to Nashville last week."

Mandie took the papers, noting the bold letters across the top. "Miss Tatum's Finishing School for Young Ladies," she read aloud. "Why, what is this for?" Her heart fluttered in fear of what it might mean.

"The school, dear, that your mother is thinking about sending you to," Mrs. Woodard replied.

Mandie sat there in shock.

Mrs. Woodard looked embarrassed. "Did you not know?" she asked.

Mandie shook her head, fighting the tears in her eyes that threatened to spill down her cheeks. "Leave home and all my friends, and go away to a strange school?" she whispered.

Uncle John walked over to Mandie and knelt beside her. "I'm sorry, Mandie. I thought your mother had discussed it with you," he said. "We've been trying to decide what's the best way for you to get your education since you live with us now."

Mandie's voice trembled. "Please, Uncle John, don't send me away," she begged. "I can go to school in Franklin."

"We talked about that, but they don't seem to teach everything your mother thinks you ought to learn," he replied.

Mrs. Woodard put her hand on Mandie's shoulder. "This school—Miss Tatum's—is one of the best schools in the southeast," she said. "Several of my friends have sent their daughters there. They all liked it, and they seemed to learn all the necessaries."

Mandie squeezed her eyes shut and swallowed hard to keep from crying.

"Put the papers with your things, Mandie, and go on back to your friends," said Uncle John, giving her a little hug. "We'll discuss this with your mother when we get back home."

"Yes, sir," was all Mandie could manage to say. She took the papers upstairs and put them in her bag, then rushed back downstairs and out onto the porch.

Liza sat alone on the steps, while Sallie and Dimar talked together on the swing and Tsa'ni played with the dogs. That meant Polly was still with Joe in the barn. But now, the sinking feeling in her stomach made her lose all interest in joining them. She flopped down on the steps beside Liza.

"Better ya git down to dat barn and see whut's goin' on," the black girl warned her.

Mandie didn't answer. She was fighting tears.

Liza frowned. "Missy, what de matter?" she asked. "You done give up on dat Mister Joe? Dat Miss Sweet Thing might jest be spreadin' some of that syrup on him."

Mandie tried to smile and took a deep breath.

"I guess they'll be back soon," Mandie replied.

"Sound like you done wore plumb out," Liza said. "Ain't got enough fight left in you to do battle."

"Liza, why did I have to ask Polly to come along anyway?" Mandie fussed.

"Yeh, I'd like to know that m'self," Liza said.

"She is my friend, but I don't like everything she does," Mandie complained. "She's such a pest. I wish I hadn't asked her to come."

But Mandie would soon regret her unkind words.

Chapter 11 / Poor Polly!

At daybreak the next morning, Joe was in the kitchen starting a fire in the big iron cookstove when he was startled by heavy pounding at the back door. Rushing to answer it, he found Morning Star and two braves standing there.

"Ned send message for John Shaw," one of the men announced.

Joe opened the door wide and asked them to come in. "Sit down. I'll get Mr. Shaw," Joe told them. He pointed to the chairs by the cookstove.

The heat felt good to the Indians. Even in the summertime the mornings were chilly.

Joe darted upstairs, but met John Shaw coming down. Uncle John had heard the pounding and came to see what was happening. Uncle Wirt and Dr. Woodard were right behind him.

"Morning Star is here with two of Uncle Ned's Indian friends. They have a message for you," Joe explained.

As John came into the kitchen, one of the Indians rose, pulled an envelope from his belt and handed it to him.

Opening it, John recognized Elizabeth's handwriting. Silently, he read:

> I am writing this for Uncle Ned. Uncle Wirt's son, Jessan, has brought him word that the bandits were seen in the woods near Asheville. There are several abandoned huts near Mr. Vanderbilt's property, and they are believed to be hiding out in one of these. Jessan said that someone found one of the long cloaks the bandits were wearing hidden in a woodpile near there. The braves and Morning Star will give you the exact directions.
>
> Uncle Ned is much better and insists on going out. Please take care of yourself, and Amanda and the others, of course.
>
> I love you. God keep you for me.
>
> Your wife,
> Elizabeth

"Look at this," John said, handing the note to Dr. Woodard. Realizing Uncle Wirt could not read English, he gave him the details.

"Must go at once," Uncle Wirt said.

Joe sprang into action. "I'll wake the girls and Dimar and Tsa'ni."

Racing up the stairs, he pounded on the door where the four girls were sleeping. Then he burst into the room where the other boys were.

"Hey, everybody, get up! We gotta go! Uncle Ned knows where the bandits are!" Joe yelled.

Dimar and Tsa'ni, already dressed, rushed downstairs.

Mandie stuck her head out of the room. "We'll be right down!" she called.

Hearing the noise, Joe's mother came out of her room and hurried to investigate. Joe followed her down the steps.

Mandie pulled her dress over her head. "Just think, we've almost caught up with them. It won't be long now," she said.

"I wonder how my grandfather knew where they are," Sallie said.

"Yo' grandfather know everything, Miss Sallie," Liza told her. "He got eyes in de back of his haid."

The four girls laughed, and hurriedly finished dressing.

"This is getting exciting," Polly squealed. She turned her back for Liza to button her dress. "Let's hurry."

"Bring your bags," Mandie told them. "Joe said we had to go." She snatched Snowball from the bed, grabbed her bag and rushed out of the room. The others followed.

Mandie led the way as the girls raced down the stairs. Then suddenly there was a scream and Polly tumbled down on top of the others. Mandie, Sallie, and Liza managed to catch themselves, but Polly fell several steps before she could stop.

The pain showed on her face. "Oh, I must've broken something!" she wailed, rubbing her ankle.

Dr. Woodard rushed to the stairway and examined the girl's foot.

He shook his head. "It looks like you've got a nasty sprain in that ankle," he said.

"Oh, no!" Polly moaned.

The doctor picked her up, carried her down the steps, past the anxious faces below, and set her on a chair by Morning Star.

"Sprained ankle," he said to John. "Let me get my bag."

The doctor quickly bathed Polly's foot in a strong-smelling liniment. As he began to bandage her ankle, the girl winced with pain.

"You won't be able to walk on that for a few days," he told her.

"Of all the luck! What will I do?" Polly asked.

Morning Star patted her hand and said, "I take home."

"Home? But I don't want to go home. I want to see those bandits when we catch them!" Polly protested.

"I'm afraid you'll have to go home, or else stay here a few days 'till it heals," the doctor told her. "It will be a miserable trip back over the mountain."

"I am sorry, Polly," Sallie told her. "My grandmother will help you to get home."

"But I don't want to go home," Polly argued. She turned to Uncle John and asked, "Can't I go on with y'all?"

"Polly, I'm sorry but I don't think that would be a good idea. Your ankle will be painful for a few days, and we may be going into a rough part of the woods," he answered. "Morning Star will be going back to my house and you can go with her. I'll send Liza back with you, if you like."

When Liza heard this, her mouth dropped open. Here they were, getting near the bandits, and now she would have to give up the excitement to go home with Miss Sweet Thing. Like Miss Amanda said, why did they ever bring her in the first place?

After a quick breakfast, Mandie and Liza talked out in the yard.

"I jest don't like dat girl," Liza grumbled, throwing her blanket over the pony. "And now here she breaks up my tea party."

Mandie grinned at her friend. "I'm glad she has to go home. You'll be doing me a favor, getting her out of my way," she said.

Liza tossed her head and laughed. "Yeh, I guess you be right, Missy. I'll take dat Miss Sweet Thing right back home so she can't chase yo' Mister Joe no mo'. But she oughta not acome in the first place. She ain't nothin' but trouble."

Mandie avoided Polly until the Indians were ready to leave. Then she waved good-bye as Polly rode off with Morning Star, Liza, and the two braves. She stared after them for a long time, relieved to see Polly go. She knew she was jealous and shouldn't be happy over her friend's misfortune, but she kept telling herself it was better this way. After all, Polly had her own accident. Mandie had nothing to do with it.

Some time later, loaded with food and good wishes from the Woodards, the group, led by Uncle Wirt and Uncle John, once again continued their journey. Joe stayed close to Mandie, with Snowball on her shoulder, and Sallie and Dimar rode right behind them. Tsa'ni brought up the rear as usual. *There is something wrong with that boy,* Mandie thought. *He always stays far behind the rest of us. He doesn't talk much and what he does say is argumentative. Why did he even come along?*

Uncle Wirt took a shortcut he knew—up mountainsides, down inclines, across rivers, and through thick underbrush. Mandie began to wonder if they'd ever get there. Suddenly an Indian on horseback appeared out of nowhere and waited on the trail ahead of them.

Mandie squinted in the bright sunshine. Instantly, a big smile spread across her face. Digging her heels into the sides of her pony, she raced around the men ahead of her. She ignored their yells to slow down. Nothing could stop her. Catching up with the Indian rider, she got close enough to grab one of his wrinkled old hands.

"Uncle Ned! Uncle Ned!" she cried. "What are you doing out here? We left you in bed."

The old man smiled at her and said, "Gold bad luck. Come see gold not make bad luck for Jim Shaw's Papoose. I promise him."

Just then Sallie rode up, looking very concerned. The other men and boys gathered around too, demanding to know why the old Indian had left his sickbed and come riding through the mountains like this.

"No more sick," Uncle Ned insisted. "Go find bad men." He patted his bow and arrows slung over his shoulder, and slipped down from his horse. "But now, time to eat," he said, finding a place to sit by the cool, tinkling stream.

Mandie sat down by him with her food, while Snowball curled up in the grass at her feet. "I've been thinking about what you told me, Uncle Ned—about tithing," Mandie told him. "God must be giving us blessings in advance. So much has happened. Tsa'ni was not killed when he fell off the railroad tracks. And you didn't die when the baggage car crashed. We have a lot to be thankful for already. Can there possibly be more?"

"Big God love Papoose," the old man said. "She ask. He answer."

"Yes, I'm thankful for all the prayers He has answered," Mandie said. "And I pray that this chase will soon be over. We have to get the gold back so we can make our tithe."

Mandie sat staring at the clear, sparkling stream as Joe came up to join them. "Did Polly get home all right, Uncle Ned?" he asked.

"Yes, foot big," the old Indian answered, holding up

his hands to illustrate. "Sore."

"I imagine it had swelled pretty badly by the time she got home," said Joe. "Too bad she got hurt and couldn't go the rest of the way with us."

Mandie fought the jealousy that rose inside of her. "I don't think Polly should have come in the first place," she said. "She's not used to this kind of life. She has been brought up in town as a lady. She can't take the rough ordeals we get into sometimes."

"Oh, give her a chance," Joe argued. "She has to learn."

"Well, this was too long a trip for her to learn on. Let her learn something somewhere else," Mandie retorted.

"Mandie!" Joe exclaimed. "You ought to be ashamed of yourself talking about your friend like that."

"She's no friend of mine!" Mandie shot back.

"Mandie!" scolded Joe.

Uncle Ned smiled, looked at the two of them, and said, "Papoose got jealous streak for Joe."

Mandie's face turned red as Joe whirled to look at her. Grinning, he said, "Is that so, Mandie? Then you must think more of me than I thought you did."

Mandie jumped up and headed toward her pony. "It's time to go," she called back, picking up Snowball on her way.

Joe ran to catch up with her. Putting his hands on her shoulders, he turned her around to face him.

"Mandie, you don't have to be jealous of Polly," he said. "She's just a friend, that's all."

Mandie shook free from his grasp. "Oh, yeh," she replied sarcastically. She mounted her pony.

As the others got ready to move, Sallie rode up beside Mandie. Having witnessed the scene between Joe and

Mandie, she tried to relieve the tension. "I would like to ride beside you, Mandie, so we can talk," she said.

"Of course, Sallie. Come on."

Riding off behind the men, the two girls talked back and forth about nothing in particular, but carefully avoided the topic of Joe. Finally Mandie decided to tell Sallie about the school in Nashville. She hadn't said a word about it to anyone else. She was hoping that somehow she wouldn't have to go.

"Sallie, do you know what my mother is planning?" she asked. "She is planning to send me away to school—far away from home."

"Oh, Mandie!" Sallie cried. "You will have to leave all your friends and your nice home?"

"Right. Mrs. Woodard gave me some papers for Mother," Mandie explained. "Mother had asked her to find out about a place called Miss Tatum's Finishing School, way out in Nashville."

"Do you have to go?" the Indian girl asked.

Mandie brushed a branch out of her way. "I don't know," she replied. "I told Uncle John I didn't want to. He said we'd talk about it with Mother when we got home. I don't want to leave all my friends and family to live at some school where I don't know anyone. That name sounds silly anyway. Imagine going to a 'finishing' school. Everyone would laugh at me."

"I would not laugh at you. I would feel sorry for you," Sallie told her. "Why can you not go to school in Franklin where you live now?"

"That's what I asked Uncle John, but he said they didn't teach some things my mother wants me to learn. I can't imagine what things they are, but I know I'd rather go to school at home where my friends are," Mandie said.

"I have heard that some of the girls enjoy going to these schools away off," Sallie told her. "They make new friends."

"I don't want to leave my mother and Uncle John and Liza and Aunt Lou and everybody. I'd even have to leave Uncle Ned. He couldn't come to a girls' school to watch over me," Mandie said.

"You do not know my grandfather," Sallie laughed. "He promised to watch over you, and nothing will keep him from doing that."

"It would be a hardship on him. He'd have to find a place to stay in Nashville. He couldn't very well stay at the school, and it'd be too far away for him to go back and forth," Mandie replied. She looked at her friend pleadingly. "Please hope and pray that I won't have to go."

"I will," Sallie promised. "Now I understand why you have been so upset since we got to Doctor Woodard's house."

"Upset? You mean you could tell it?" Mandie asked.

"Yes, you have not been as cheerful as usual," Sallie answered. "I believe you hurt Joe's feelings back there, but I understand now."

Mandie's eyes widened. "Hurt *Joe's* feelings? *He* got mad at *me*!" she said defensively.

"Did he? I think *you* caused the problem by criticizing your friend, Polly," Sallie told her bluntly. "Of course, it's none of my business, but I hate to see my friends angry with each other."

"You think I caused it?" Mandie asked, trying to remember exactly what she and Joe had said.

"Yes," Sallie replied. "I heard my grandfather say you were jealous, and I agree with him. Think about it, Mandie. You and Joe have been close friends all your lives. Suddenly Polly meets Joe and decides she likes him, too. That is enough to make anyone jealous."

Mandie frowned in bewilderment. "Then, what should I have said or done?" she asked.

"Just ignore Polly's attitude toward Joe," Sallie advised. "She will become disenchanted sooner or later. I think she is only flitting about. She is not serious about anyone or anything. That is just her personality. Some people are like that."

Mandie knew her friend was right. "Thanks for your advice, Sallie," she said. "I guess I have been mean, and I'm really sorry. I'll have to do something about it."

At the next rest stop, when they dismounted, Mandie walked over to Joe, smiled apologetically, and reached for his hand. "Joe, could we take a little walk?" she asked.

Joe was happy to see his friend smile. "Sure, Mandie," he replied with a big grin. "Let's walk down the stream a little ways."

They strolled silently for several minutes, then stopped to watch the tiny cricket frogs hopping along the edge of the stream.

As they stood close together, Mandie faced Joe and swallowed with difficulty. "Joe, please forgive me for acting like I did about Polly," she said. "I'm really sorry. I won't do it again."

Joe turned to face her, and smiled. "It's all forgiven, Mandie. I understand," he told her. "I've been riding next to your Uncle John. He told me that you were upset because they were thinking about sending you away to school. I don't blame you. I'd be upset, too. In fact, *I'd* just plain rebel."

"Oh, Joe, it would be awful to leave everyone and go away by myself to some strange place with strange people," she told him, petting Snowball on her shoulder. "I just couldn't stand it."

"I'm sorry, Mandie. If I can do anything to help you out, I will," Joe promised. "I don't want you to go away either. I'd hardly ever get to see you."

"I know. I'd probably only get to come home for holidays, and there aren't many of them," Mandie said. Tears glistened in her blue eyes. "I just don't know what to do."

Joe pulled the bandana from around his neck and wiped away her tears.

"Don't cry, Mandie. We'll think up some way to get out of it," he said. "Maybe when your mother sees how you feel, she won't make you go."

"Maybe," Mandie said. "But she really wants me to learn how to be a proper lady."

"A proper lady?" Joe laughed. "That's funny. I thought you were a proper lady already."

Mandie giggled. "You know what she means. She wants me to learn how to put on the social airs."

"I'm not so sure I want my future wife to learn all that nonsense," Joe told her. "You might get so you think you're better than I am."

Mandie jerked his hand. "Don't ever say that! That will never happen! You know that!"

"Let's hope it doesn't!" Joe said.

Rejoining the rest of the group, Joe and Mandie continued on their gold-recovery mission. But, somehow, they had to find a way for Mandie to get out of going to Miss Tatum's Finishing School.

Chapter 12 / The Creatures in the Woods

As the group got a glimpse of the wealthy Mr. Vanderbilt's mansion in the distance, Uncle Ned held his hand up signaling them to halt.

"Must be quiet. Go slow now," he told them. "Into woods." He pointed to a faint trail leading off to the left from the main road.

They followed him into the dark woods. The sun sank lower in the sky, and thick trees blocked out most of the remaining daylight.

The old Indian stopped in the thick underbrush and dismounted. "Leave horses here," he said. "Bring rope, bow, arrows."

"Joe, we must be awfully close now," Mandie whispered excitedly.

"Yes, and you stay back," he whispered, slinging his rifle over his shoulder. "I'll go ahead with the men."

Mandie took Snowball in her arms as she and Joe joined the group around Uncle Ned. Dimar stood ready with one hand on his bow and arrows and the other on his rifle. Tsa'ni trailed along behind.

Uncle John spoke in a loud whisper. "We will move

forward slowly," he explained. "And when we spot the cabin, you young people stay back out of sight."

"I would like to go with you," Dimar volunteered.

"We'll probably need you boys later, but let us men handle things first," Uncle John answered. "We'll let you know what we're going to do."

They crept quietly through the woods until they came within sight of an old rickety cabin. Uncle Wirt pointed to the woodpile nearby. Running over to it, he held up one of the long cloaks the bandits had worn. It was just as Uncle Wirt's son, Jessan, had said.

There were three horses tied behind the hut, and an old wagon stood in front. The strong odor of fish cooking filled the air, and a faint sound of voices came from inside the hut. There were no windows in the hut—only one door, and it was standing open.

Uncle Ned slipped behind a tree on one side of the cabin, and Uncle Wirt moved into position on the other side. Uncle John hid behind a tree between the other two. The young people huddled together where they were, waiting breathlessly.

Suddenly Snowball jumped down from Mandie's shoulder and darted for the door of the hut. Mandie caught her breath and froze. When the kitten stepped into the clearing around the cabin, they all watched and waited anxiously.

Snowball walked straight through the doorway of the cabin. Immediately, there was a big commotion inside. The cat meowed loudly. "Hey, come hyar, you cat!" a gruff voice hollered.

Snowball ran out the door with a big, burly man close behind. He stooped and grabbed the kitten. Snowball started biting and scratching. The man shook him violently.

"You dumb cat! Bite, will you? I'll kill you for that!" he yelled.

The kitten managed to get loose, but instead of returning to Mandie, he ran in circles around the clearing. The man grabbed an axe from the woodpile and chased the cat furiously.

Mandie could stand it no more. She had to save her kitten. Breaking quickly through the underbrush before anyone could stop her, she ran into the clearing, intent on rescuing Snowball.

When the bandit saw her, he whirled and started in her direction. "How did you git hyar?" he bellowed. "Hey, you're that gal on the train with that cat, ain't you?" he said as he got closer.

Mandie began to chase Snowball, and the man chased her. Then, all of a sudden, a sharp arrow whizzed across the clearing and grazed the bandit's leg. He screamed and fell to the ground, clasping his bleeding leg.

A second man edged out of the hut to see what was going on. Uncle Ned and Uncle John rushed forward and knocked him down. With Uncle Wirt's help they tied him and the wounded man to a tree away from the clearing.

The third man, still inside the hut, called out. "What's goin' on out there?" There was no answer. He came to the doorway. But when he saw the others in the yard, he slammed and barred the door.

Mandie hurried with Snowball to the shelter of the trees. "Snowball, why do you always have to cause trouble?" she scolded.

Uncle John summoned the boys. "All right, come on if you want to help," he said.

The boys followed quickly.

"How are we going to get that man out of the cabin?" Joe asked.

"We can shoot him out," Uncle John suggested. "The cabin has enough holes in it to shoot through. Or we can just wait for him to come out. He has to, sooner or later," he said as the two old Indians joined them.

"Why do we not burn him out?" Tsa'ni asked.

"Burn him out? Suppose the gold is in that cabin and it burns up," Dimar protested.

"Gold wouldn't burn up," Uncle John informed him.

"Fire dangerous!" Uncle Wirt added.

"I agree," said Uncle John. "He doesn't really have a chance. We're all armed. The odds are in our favor. Everyone get your weapons ready. I think we can get him to surrender."

As soon as the bows and arrows and rifles were aimed and ready, Uncle John called to the man inside. "Come out!" he said. "We've got you completely surrounded, and we are armed."

There was no answer. Everyone waited silently, their weapons pointed at the only door of the old shack.

Mandie and Sallie remained at a distance, watching and biting their fingernails, afraid someone would get hurt.

Slowly, the door to the cabin opened, and the last bandit, seeing all their weapons, hurried out into the yard.

"Don't shoot! I give up!" he called as the men and boys advanced.

Quickly, Uncle Ned threw his rope around the bandit, and Uncle Wirt helped tie him up. After leaving him with the other two, Uncle Ned and Uncle Wirt joined the others.

"All right, let's go find the gold," Joe said, leading the way into the cabin.

The girls started to come forward and follow, but Uncle Ned waved them back.

"Stay!" he called to them, as he, too, entered the hut.

Mandie took the rope she was carrying and let one end dangle so that Snowball could play with it. Worry clouded her face. "What if they don't find the gold in there, Sallie?" she asked. "Those men might've spent it."

Sallie laughed. "I do not think they could spend that much gold so soon."

Snowball scratched around at Sallie's feet, throwing dirt everywhere.

The Indian girl looked down. "Why does Snowball keep scratching in the dirt?"

"I don't know," Mandie answered. "Snowball, please be still."

Then she saw what the kitten was playing with. It looked like a string, but when she stooped to pick it up, it wouldn't come all the way out. Part of it was buried under the ground. The more Mandie pulled at it, the more excited she became.

"Sallie, look!" she cried. "This string is attached to something underground!"

Sallie knelt beside her. "Do you think it could be one of the drawstrings on the bags of gold?" she asked.

"Oh, I hope so," Mandie replied as both girls started digging with their hands.

They were right. Within minutes they had uncovered one of the bags of gold. And from the looks of the tangled web of strings, it appeared that the other bags were there, too.

Mandie picked up Snowball and the bag of gold. "Let's

get Uncle Ned!" she exclaimed, heading for the cabin. Sallie stayed right behind her.

As they got to the doorway, Mandie shouted. "Uncle Ned, we've found it!" They all stopped their searching and gathered around her. "It's buried out there where we've been standing all this time," she said, laughing.

With everyone helping it didn't take long to uncover the rest of the gold. After loading it into the old wagon in front of the cabin, they hitched up two of the bandits' horses. Then they brought the bandits back into the clearing and made them get into the wagon.

Uncle John looked at them with great satisfaction. "We're taking you into town and turning you over to the authorities," he said.

"Mister, please don't do that," one of them begged. "You've got yer gold back. Jest let us go."

Uncle John climbed in beside them. "How did you happen to know about the gold anyway?" he asked.

"Well, it's sorta like this. We got some friends you'ins knows. Rennie Lou and Snuff. They still in that thar jail but we'ins got out. They was the ones what told us about the gold," one of the bandits replied.

"Then we just hung around 'til we found out what you was gonna do with it. I acted like an ol' drunken bum and laid in that thar alley behind the bank in Bryson City while you'ins were loadin' it up," he said proudly. "I heard the whole plan."

"Oh, hesh up!" yelled one of the other bandits.

"Rennie Lou and Snuff," Uncle John repeated. "The man and woman who kidnapped Mandie, Joe, and Sallie in the mountains and then tried to burn down your barn, Uncle Ned. Remember, we took them into town and turned them over to the law."

"Bad people," Uncle Ned said. "These bad people, too."

"Take to jail," Uncle Wirt told him.

So that's what they did. On the way into town, the young people rode their ponies behind the men, while Uncle Ned drove the wagon full of gold and bandits.

When they turned the bandits over to the jailor, he said he would summon the local doctor for the wounded man.

Then Uncle Ned headed the wagon in the direction of the huge bank in downtown Asheville.

Uncle John knew the banker, and it didn't take long to unload the gold and place it in the bank's vault. It would be safe there until they could start building the hospital for the Cherokees.

Since it was getting late and they had missed their hotel stay, thanks to the bandits, Uncle John checked them into the hotel in Asheville for the night. Early next morning they began the trip back to Franklin. Elizabeth and Morning Star would be waiting for them.

It was exciting to stay in the hotel, but Mandie was anxious to get home and tell her mother all the wonderful news. Yet on the other hand, she dreaded any further discussion of the school in Nashville.

Chapter 13 / Getting Things Settled

When the tired travelers finally reached Franklin, they found Elizabeth and Morning Star waiting for them in the parlor. "Oh, John, I'm so glad you're home," Elizabeth said, greeting her husband with a hug.

John kissed her. "We're all dirty, tired, and hungry," he replied, "but very happy to be here."

Elizabeth looked over the entire group. "You young people had better get cleaned up," she said. "Then go out in the kitchen and get a bite to eat. But after that, into bed, every one of you. You all need a nap—and no arguing."

There was no protest. Mandie's eyes sparkled. "Oh, Mother! Isn't it wonderful?" she bubbled. "The gold is safe. We finally found it. The bandits are in jail, and the gold is in the bank at Asheville!"

"I'm glad, dear." Elizabeth smiled. "We'll discuss your trip more after a while. Now go along with the others." She waved Mandie on through the doorway to clean up.

Jenny and Liza weren't around at the moment, but Aunt Lou waited for the youngsters in the kitchen. The old woman smiled and put her arms around Mandie. "My chile!" she said. "I knowed de good Lawd gonna send you back safe!"

"Aunt Lou, we found the bandits and the gold," Mandie said excitedly.

"I knowed you would." The old woman grinned. "Now, y'all jest get your food waitin' there on the stove and then git on upstairs to rest. I'se got to take some of this out to Mister John, and Mister Ned, and Mister Wirt and Miz Lizbeth."

The hungry young people gathered around the cookstove and began filling their plates, while Aunt Lou piled a large tray full of food for the adults.

Mandie and her friends could hardly hold their heads up as they ate at the kitchen table. They were too tired to talk—almost too tired to eat. They might have fallen asleep at the table had it not been for Aunt Lou's bustling in and out to wait on the adults. Aunt Lou finally sent them to bed, and they readily obeyed.

After that much-needed nap, as soon as Mandie could get away from the others, she hurried over to Polly's house. She had to make things right with her friend.

Polly sat on her front porch with her foot propped up on a stool. "Hello, Mandie," Polly greeted her. "Aunt Lou told our cook that y'all had got home. Do sit down and tell me what happened."

Mandie related the details of their trip to her friend and then fell silent.

"There's something you aren't telling me, Mandie," Polly said.

"Yes, there is," Mandie replied, twisting around in her chair. Her heart pounded as she tried to find the right words. "I don't know how to explain it, but I've had some bad feelings toward you, and I want to ask your forgiveness for being rude."

"Bad feelings toward me? When?" Polly asked in surprise. "And how can I forgive something that I don't even know about?"

"I suppose—I got a little jealous of, uh, of you and Joe," Mandie faltered.

"Me and Joe? That's funny." Polly laughed.

"And then when you hurt your foot, I was glad you had to go home," Mandie confessed. "Will you forgive me?"

Polly looked as though she couldn't believe it. "You were glad I had to go home? But then, why did you ask me to go along in the first place?" she asked.

"Because you're my friend," Mandie told her. "It probably doesn't make sense to you, but will you please forgive me?"

"Sure, Mandie," she said. "I know I talked like I was brave, but I have to confess I was getting tired of all that running around all over the mountain. And I sure didn't want to come face to face with those bandits. So you see, I was glad to come home, but I didn't want anyone to know it."

Mandie giggled. "Oh, Polly, I'm sorry," she said. "I am so glad for your friendship, and I wouldn't want to do anything to spoil it."

Polly changed the subject. "Guess what? My mother is sending me away to school," she told Mandie.

"No!" Mandie couldn't believe it. "Where?"

"All the way to Nashville," Polly replied.

"Not Miss Tatum's Finishing School for Young Ladies?" Mandie gasped.

"How did you know?" Polly asked.

"Because my mother has the same idea, but Uncle John said we'd talk it over," Mandie told her.

"You don't want to go?"

"No, I don't," Mandie said. "Don't tell me *you* really want to go."

"Oh, yes," Polly assured her. "I think that would be great fun to live at a school that far away from home."

"Well, I don't," Mandie stated flatly. "And I hope I can talk my mother out of it. I don't want to go so far away and not be able to see my friends and my family."

"My mother doesn't know that I know it, but she had other motives. You see, if I go away to school, she'll be free to travel all she wants to," Polly said. "I'll be more or less on my own, and that suits me fine. I wish you'd go, too, Mandie. We could have lots of fun together way out there away from everybody."

"Sorry, Polly, but I don't want to go. I may have to, but I'm not going without a fight," Mandie told her.

When Mandie got home, she found Uncle Ned alone on the front porch, and sat down beside him. Another matter still troubled her.

"Uncle Ned, I've been trying to figure out how we can give ten percent of the gold to the Lord," she said, leaning back on her hands.

"Cherokees make Papoose boss of gold," he said. "Papoose give tithe."

"But I mean, what can we actually do with the ten percent? Should we just give it to your church at Birdtown, or should we do something else with it?"

The old Indian thought for a moment, and then a big grin came over his wrinkled face. "Church no have music box," he told her.

Mandie smiled broadly. "Then that's what we'll do.

We'll buy the biggest, most expensive organ we can find to put in your church," she said excitedly. "Do you think the other Cherokees will agree?"

"Cherokees give gold to Papoose," Uncle Ned told her.

"Yes, but I have to use it for the good of the Cherokees," she replied. "It really belongs to them. I'm only going to spend it for their good."

"Get music box for church," the old man said, nodding his head. "That be tithe. Then watch window open and Big God throw blessings out to people."

"We have already received many blessings," Mandie said gratefully.

"More to come," Uncle Ned assured her.

Mandie leaned forward and lowered her voice. "Uncle Ned, did you know that my mother is planning to send me all the way to Nashville to a finishing school?"

"No!" he exclaimed.

"Yes, and I will have to leave all my friends and family, and go to this strange school where there are all strange people and I won't know anyone," she complained. "And worst of all, you can't go with me, or even come to visit. What will I do, Uncle Ned?"

"Not good," her old friend muttered. "Must not send Papoose so far away."

Mandie stood up. "I'm going to talk to my mother and Uncle John about it right now. I'll let you know what happens."

Mandie found her mother and Uncle John in the small sitting room adjoining their bedroom. Entering, she sat down on a footstool near her uncle.

"Uncle John, have you talked to Mother about the

school yet?" she asked, holding her breath. She feared his answer.

"That's what we've just been talking about," he replied.

"Well, what did you decide?" Mandie asked.

"That you won't be going to Nashville to school," Elizabeth answered. "However—"

"—That's good news," Mandie interrupted. "I'm so glad I don't have to leave my friends and go all the way to that strange town."

"Amanda, wait until I've finished," her mother reprimanded. "You won't be going to Nashville, because we've decided to send you to the school I attended in Asheville. It will be much closer. Also, your grandmother lives in Asheville. Remember?"

Mandie took several deep breaths to steady her voice. "But, Mother," she protested, "why do I have to go anywhere out of town? Why can't I go to school right here in Franklin?"

"The school here in Franklin doesn't teach everything you need to learn, and their standards aren't as high," Elizabeth explained. "You must be prepared for society."

"Once you get settled in and make some new friends, you'll like Asheville, dear," Uncle John tried to comfort her. "It's not very far away, and you can come home whenever you like—on weekends and holidays."

"Oh, phooey!" Mandie said in a defeated voice. "I want to live at home all the time, with you and Mother."

"But, Amanda, all girls have to be educated," her mother said. "Just be thankful that we can afford a private school."

Mandie didn't answer.

Uncle John made an attempt to smooth things over.

"Let's try it for a little while, and if you don't like it, we'll bring you home. But I really think you'll make new friends there. And you'll be able to get better acquainted with your grandmother. You know, you've only seen her once."

Mandie remembered when she met the heavyset woman in the expensive clothes. Her grandmother had not been very friendly. Mandie wondered if she could ever break through that cold wall between them.

She stood up. "I guess I have to go if you say so," she said, managing a reluctant smile. "But at least I don't have to go to Nashville."

Elizabeth looked at John as Mandie left the room. "She doesn't realize how much we'd like to have her stay home where we can be with her every day, but there are things you have to sacrifice sometimes," she told him.

"I really meant that, Elizabeth, when I told her we'd bring her home if she doesn't like the school," John reminded her.

"Yes, I agree," Elizabeth replied.

Mandie rushed back downstairs to Uncle Ned on the front porch. "Uncle Ned, I don't have to go to Nashville to school after all," she told him, excitedly.

"Papoose stay home?" he asked, smiling.

"No, not exactly," she answered. "I have to go to a school in Asheville where my mother went."

"But that not far," the old man assured her. "I go see Papoose in Asheville."

"Will you, Uncle Ned?" she asked eagerly. "I won't know anyone there and it'll be awfully lonesome."

"I promise Jim Shaw I watch over Papoose. Keep promise," the old Indian told her.

Mandie looked at him suddenly, surprise dawning on her face. "You know what? We just planned the tithe, and